Promise of Shelter

Previously Published Work

Poetry
Shadowplay, 1978
The Space Between Sleep and Waking, 1981
Three Sestinas, 1984
Anyone Skating On That Middle Ground, 1984
Becoming Light, 1987
The Touchstone: Poems New and Selected, 1992

Prose
A Nice Gazebo, 1992

Promise of Shelter

Robyn Sarah

The Porcupine's Quill

CANADIAN CATALOGUING IN PUBLICATION DATA

Sarah, Robyn, 1949-
Promise of shelter

ISBN 0-88984-192-6

I. Title.

PS8587.A3765P76 1997   C813'.54   C97-932188-3
PR9199.3.S27P76 1997

Published by The Porcupine's Quill, 68 Main Street, Erin, Ontario
NOB 1T0. Readied for the press by John Metcalf. Copy edited by
Doris Cowan. Typeset in Ehrhardt, printed on Zephyr Antique Laid,
and bound at The Porcupine's Quill Inc.

The cover is after a photograph by Chad Evans Wyatt.
The author photo is courtesy of D.R. Cowles.

This is a work of fiction. Any resemblance of characters to persons,
living or dead, is purely coincidental.

Represented in Canada by the Literary Press Group.
Trade orders are available from General Distribution Services.

We acknowledge the support of the Canada Council for the Arts
for our publishing programme. The support of the Ontario Arts
Council and the Department of Canadian Heritage through the
Book and Periodical Industry Development Programme is also
gratefully acknowledged.

1 2 3 4 · 99 98 97

Contents

Acknowledgements

The author wishes to thank the Canada Council and the Ministère des Affaires Culturelles du Québec for their support at various stages in the writing of these stories.

* * *

Stories from this collection were first published or accepted for publication (sometimes in slightly different versions) in the following periodicals and anthologies:

'Unlit Water' in *Prairie Schooner* and in *Future Tense: New English Fiction from Quebec*; 'Accept My Story' in *The Malahat Review* and in *The Journey Prize Anthology 6*; 'Janine' in *The Malahat Review* and in *A Room at the Heart of Things*; 'Looking For My Keys' in *Canadian Fiction Magazine*; 'Shelter' and 'At My Left Hand Gabriel' in *The New Quarterly*; 'The Paper Knife' in *The Massachusetts Review*; and 'Deuxième Arabesque' (under the title 'Passing the Solstice') in *Quarterly West*.

For D, who meets me halfway.

Unlit Water

THERE WERE GRANDSTAND seats for the fireworks at La Ronde, but you had to pay for those. Everywhere else, it was a free show. For two weeks running, every other night, droves headed down towards the river, just before dark, to some choice vantage point – the Jacques Cartier Bridge, closed to traffic, for those who came early enough; the space underneath the bridge for the overflow; various points along the waterfront for others.

'Let's go,' said Miriam on the fourth or fifth night. 'We haven't been yet this year. The whole block is going. The kids want to go.' She stood on the steps of the screened porch, holding her hair up off her neck with one hand, doubling a ponytail holder anchored between her teeth with the other. She was looking down at the damp back of Allan's T-shirt as he bent over his partially disassembled bicycle on the strip of cracked cement that was still this building's excuse for a backyard. When the breeze wafted upward, she could smell his sweat.

'You go,' said Allan without looking up, his arm muscle flexing as he struggled with a stubborn bolt. 'We went enough last year. I don't even particularly like fireworks.'

She laughed. 'How can you *not like* fireworks?'

'You've seen them once, it's enough.'

It was the sort of remark of his she'd used to find funny. But in a way she knew what he meant; it *was* sort of a bizarre idea – an annual, international fireworks festival, a full fifty minutes of fireworks, night after night. It was like birthday cake every day. Still, Montrealers seemed anything but sated.

Trying a different tack, she said, 'You promised Jonah.'

'When did I?'

'In the car, on the way home from school. When he said everyone in his class has been at least once.'

'I said we'd go *sometime*. I never said tonight.'

'But there are only a couple nights left, and we can't go on the weekend – we have that birthday dinner for Liz's sister.'

'Look, I told you, you want to take them, go without me.' The edge of irritation in his voice made her not inclined to pursue it. She didn't know how to tell him, and she didn't want to tell him, that she was afraid to go by herself – that the crowds made her nervous, that she wasn't sure how to get to where they'd watched from last year, that she was afraid of losing her way, of losing a child in the throng (Susannah sometimes refused to hold hands, these days), generally of not being able to deal with the situation on her own. It was a way that she felt more and more often. What situation? he would want to know, and she asked herself now. What's the big deal? You get on the bus and metro like a half-million other people, families with their strollers and blankets and tote-bags and folding chairs, and you follow the crowd. How can you get lost? It doesn't matter where you end up – you can see the fireworks from anyplace down there. Still, she balked.

In the alley beyond the back gate, voices shouted back and forth. 'Aren't we going to the fireworks? Isn't it time?' 'Where's Randy?' 'He went with Marc-Antoine and Marc-Antoine's dad. They've left already.' '*Sébastien, viens! Liliane!*' A flurry of running footsteps, cries, back doors slamming. Next door a telephone rang and rang. The alley was emptying of children.

The sky was overcast, the June air close and humid. It was beginning to get dark. Faint lightning flickered above the roof-tops, and somebody yelled, 'Hey, they're starting!' Miriam glanced at her watch; nine-twenty. It wasn't the fireworks; they never started before ten, though a flare or two might go off, five minutes till, to prime the crowd. Somewhere down the block, a police siren bleeped and warbled, the sound getting stuck, swallowing itself, then lurching out again, idiot noise. There was more lightning.

'It's going to rain, anyway,' said Allan. He put down his wrench with a clatter. 'Are the kids' bikes locked up?'

'No, they're still riding them. Out front.'

'Well, better go call them.'

But she didn't have to; Jonah's head peered down from the balcony above. 'Mom!'

'Where's Susannah? What did you do with your bikes?'

'She's here, Mom. We left them under the front stairs. Mom! Uncle Barry says he'll *drive* us to the fireworks. He says there's room, Auntie Liz doesn't want to come. We can all fit.'

For confirmation, Barry's head appeared too. 'Ahoy! Brother of mine! Shall we wend our way down to the harbour with the rest of town?'

'Allan thinks it's going to rain.'

'Nah. That's heat lightning. If it does, it'll just be a drizzle.'

'I give up,' said Allan. 'Okay, we'll go. Let me put this stuff away. I'll meet you out front.'

Miriam ran to collect windbreakers, a blanket, a snack. Into a plastic bag she threw what she could find, the fridge was nearly empty, three plums, a hard nectarine, an apple; a few bran muffins left over from breakfast, the overdone ones, crumbling where burnt parts had stuck when she forked them out of the tin.

'Go change into long pants,' she told the children, who were in shorts. 'It's windy by the water.'

'We don't need to,' called Jonah, running down the hall towards the front door. 'There isn't time.'

He was seven; Susannah was four. A year ago they had still taken their baths together. They had two-wheelers,

Susannah's with training wheels she insisted she didn't need any more. Her hair was cut short, almost like his. Miriam had done them both. She hadn't meant to take so much off Susannah's. The backs of their necks were soft, sweet-smelling, still babyish.

'Go to the bathroom, though!' she yelled after them.

The traffic wasn't bad. Barry eased the car (his car; Allan shared it) into a cobbled laneway between buildings, some-where in Old Montreal, and they got out, squeezing between other vehicles, and began to walk down towards the water. They merged with a broad, slow stream of walkers: cyclists wheeling their bikes, lovers arm in arm, fathers with small children on their shoulders, mothers pushing strollers, col-lege students already half soused, arms linked, singing. 'Hold my hand,' she told Susannah. 'And don't let go.' Jonah was ahead, walking between Barry and Allan. He had on an Expos cap, his cowlick sticking out crookedly above the strap. The crowd seemed to press in, surging forward by increments, carrying them along.

It was 1986. It was the year that an American space shuttle called the Challenger exploded, moments after lift-off, presumably vaporizing everyone aboard – among them a young woman schoolteacher from New Hampshire whose own children, along with millions across North America, were watching the launch on TV. Millions saw the white vapour trail suddenly veer to one side, loop crazily, and fun-nel out, twister-style, before it trailed off in a few puffs of white smoke. Millions, wondering, heard the announcers' voices falter and stumble, confirming that something seemed to have gone wrong. In school auditoriums across the United States, balloons and flags were still waving.

Miriam felt raindrops on her bare arms. 'Mom,' said

Jonah, suddenly at her elbow, 'If it rains hard, will they counsel the fireworks?'

'*Cancel*,' she corrected absently. 'It won't. It's just a drizzle. Do you want your windbreaker?'

He didn't. 'If it *pours*, I mean.'

Susannah said in a prim, authoritative voice, looking around, 'If it pours, we will all get *soaking wet*.'

She gave them each a plum from her bag, and ate one herself. She ate a dry, crumbly muffin. They were at the waterfront now. 'Let's stop and look at the ships,' said Barry. 'Come, Susannah girl, you want a lift up?' People were clustered along the railing, but they managed to squeeze themselves in and find a spot for Jonah. He climbed on the lower rail and held on to the upper, craning forward. She kept a hand on his shirt collar.

A row of freighters sat motionless on the water, in frontal view, their hulls immense, towering. One of them, taller than the rest, stood out. In the unreal light of the vapour lamps, its black sides, pocked with rust, gleamed faintly. She read the name: ROMANIA. For some reason she shivered. The height of the thing surprised her, and the somehow frightening immediacy of it. It was like a ship in a bad dream.

'Dad!' Jonah cried sharply. He scrambled down from the railing. 'I don't like that big boat. It's scary.'

'Bit of an awesome sight, isn't it, from this angle,' remarked Allan. He put an arm around his son's shoulder, and they walked slowly on.

Susannah was having a ride. 'Uncle Barry,' she said suddenly, peering down at the top of his head, 'You've got a hole in your hair now, just like my dad's.'

'Barry! Is that true?' Allan was surprised.

'I'm afraid so.' Barry reached up and tweaked Susannah's ear. 'That's Uncle Barry's secret, love,' he said reproachfully. 'Cover it back up for me, will you?'

He was nearly five years younger, he was thirty-four. Liz that spring had had another miscarriage, her fourth. The first was just after they'd all bought the duplex together, when Susannah was a baby. He didn't talk about it, Liz didn't. This year she had decided to go back to school and do her Ph.D. They renovated their kitchen, they gave parties. They travelled. Barry taught English as a second language; they could get postings anywhere. In September they were going to China.

Miriam knew Allan envied the travelling. He had dreamed of being a photojournalist. He'd lost a good job when the *Montreal Star*, the larger of two English-language dailies, shut down overnight, the year Jonah was born. At the time, the wage settlement of a full year's salary had seemed a bonanza, a chance to prove what he could really do. No big break had come – only little breaks – only enough so they'd been able to salt away part of that settlement for a down payment on the duplex, just before real estate prices in the neighbourhood went sky high. This year, with the tax increase, he'd had to supplement his freelance income doing weddings and school pictures. Even with her replacement teaching, they just met expenses. Nothing over, not even enough to rip down the old back shed and break up the cement and make a real backyard as they'd talked of doing ... certainly nothing for vacation or travel. He never complained, but he talked less and less, and often, lately, she woke in the night and found him not in bed. He'd be sitting in the lighted kitchen in his bathrobe, sandy-eyed, flipping through a magazine; or he'd have nodded off sitting up in the den, to the flicker of the late-late movie. He had begun smoking again, and this time she didn't say anything about it.

The rain had stopped. A series of muffled explosions drew scattered cheers and whistles from the crowd.

'They're starting!' sang Susannah.

'No,' said Jonah. '*Soon* they're starting, is what that means. When they're *really* starting, the light on the Ferris wheel goes out. Is it out, Susannah?'

'No,' she replied from her perch.

'Can't we get closer?' asked Miriam. 'Can't we get somewhere more open, where the kids can see? There must be someplace we can sit down.'

They were passing the grassy island where they'd watched most of last year's shows, but it was full. There wasn't a square foot of grass to be seen. Families had come early and installed themselves, with their blankets, lawn chairs, thermoses; whole rafts of them it seemed, different ethnic groups, grandparents, uncles, cousins. She wondered briefly if it was mostly immigrants who came to see the fireworks. Now they saw that the harbour quay, too, was full. Same story: the chairs lined up along the water, men with their six-packs open, children dodging in and out among the grownups, perched on the railings, calling to one another in various languages.

'I have an idea,' said Barry. 'Follow me.'

Hurrying now, they squeezed through dark throngs of people who had stopped moving, and soon found themselves skirting a chain link fence, back of an abandoned factory. Further along there was a break in it, a bent and flattened part, as though a truck had rammed it; at its lowest it was easily gotten over. On the other side was a wide concrete embankment with unobstructed access to the water. Comparatively few people had found their way onto it so far; they could see large empty spaces.

'Are we allowed in here?'

'Well, we aren't the only ones,' said Barry. He stopped to set Susannah down, his arm brushing Miriam's. The factory loomed above them, a vast empty structure, some of its windows boarded, others yawning. In a few, high up, shards of glass glinted darkly, reflecting the faint available light. The sky was purplish. A smear of moon showed through murky cloud cover.

'I don't think I've ever seen one of these old factories close up,' said Miriam. 'It's like something out of a De Chirico painting.'

Barry said, 'They spook me. I find them evil. It's like the very walls go on sweating the misery of the workers who passed their lives in there. Generations of them.' A wind came up as he spoke, and she smelled the river.

Another battery of explosions went off, and three pink flares soared up from the island fairground across the water. The sounds of cheering drifted raggedly across the dark, from the scattered arenas, strangely high-pitched, unreal.

The children were excited. They ran ahead, tugging at Allan, who had the blanket; they wanted him to get a spot right by the water. People had begun to line up along the edge, some with their legs hanging over. There was no railing here, and as she came closer Miriam saw that the retaining ledge they sat on was only a couple of inches high. Over the edge, at a drop of four or five feet, was black water, deep enough for ships. It was much darker here than along the festooned harbour quay. The inky surface had little to reflect, but here and there faint glimmers betrayed the movement of currents.

'Right here will be fine,' Allan was saying as he spread the blanket on the rough cement, a few feet from the edge.

'Daddy, why not right on the edge? People could go in front of us, here.'

'You'll still see fine, don't worry.'

'Why *not*, Dad?'

'This is close enough,' said Miriam firmly. 'This is plenty close. There's no railing.' She sat down beside Barry in the dark, pulling Susannah between them. 'Jonah,' she warned, he was hopping up and down in protest, 'You sit down, too.' People were still moving in on all sides, finding places for themselves. A young couple, Latin-looking, the woman carrying a girl of about two, stepped across the blanket between Miriam and Allan, excusing themselves, and sat down on the ledge in front. The woman turned back and smiled at Miriam, apologetic. She was very pretty, and as she settled the little girl onto her lap and leaned comfortably against her husband, he bent forward and kissed her on the temple.

I'd never sit on the edge like that with such a young child, Miriam thought, she's crazy. Suppose the little girl gets restless and starts to jump around, she could lose her hold. Suppose they get jostled. As if in answer to her thought, a burst of raucous laughter rose a little to the left of where they were sitting; a group of young men, boys, some in leather jackets, were throwing something around, no, they were juggling, with unopened beer cans. '*Bravo! Hé, tabernac!*' She heard cans opening, fizzing over, more laughter and swearing.

If a child fell in here, what could anybody do about it? What could even the most powerful of swimmers do, in the dark, in that unlit stretch of black water? Who could you call on for help? It would be the end, in seconds, utterly without recourse. One minute you could be watching the fireworks, and the next, the bottom could have fallen out of your life.

'Allan.' She couldn't see his face, he was looking in the direction of La Ronde. 'Allan, let's get up and move back a little, can we? We're really close to the edge. Allan?' She leaned over to touch his arm.

'What are you talking about?' he said, turning, peering at her in the dimness. 'We're a good six feet from the edge.'

'I know, but the kids can't swim. If people get rowdy ... If there were a fight...' She leaped to her feet suddenly as though she'd been shot. '*Where's Jonah?*'

'Miriam, *take it easy*!' said Barry in a voice of pained consternation. 'He's standing right behind you.'

Her heart had risen to her throat and was hammering there. 'Jonah, for heaven's sake, *sit down*! Sit down on the blanket and stay sitting! Susannah, *you too*!' She pulled them both down roughly beside her, gripping their wrists, hurting Susannah, who wailed.

'Mom, what's the matter?' Jonah said, wondering. 'Why can't we stand up? We can't fall in. We're *far away* from the edge.' Cheers rose again as the light on the Ferris wheel went out.

She couldn't name or explain the dread that had come over her, the cold trembling that seemed to have its source in the pit of her stomach and to radiate out from there in waves. She knew that it was madness for them to be where they were, for her to have taken so lightly the idea that they come here in the first place, to watch fireworks; and she knew it was hopeless to try to get Allan or Barry to understand. Almost crying, she felt that all she wanted in the world was to pull up stakes, to move back and keep moving back, to pick up their blanket and tow it safely away from the water. But people had piled up in a dense wall behind them now, and the fireworks were beginning.

Shelter

AT A QUARTER TO ELEVEN on a January night Holly Bailey, a single mother, realized that there was no milk left in the house for breakfast, and slipped out to buy some at the convenience store a block away.

Just outside the front door she hesitated, for she thought she heard one of the boys wake up, but after a moment there was silence and she guessed he had only sighed or spoken a word aloud in his sleep, as both of them sometimes did. She never liked leaving them at night, even for the few moments it took to run to the store and back, and she rarely did it; but their schoolbus came at an unholy 7:15 in the morning, before any of the nearby stores opened. She knew they would want their usual cereal for breakfast, and would balk at the idea of eating anything else.

Quietly locking the door behind her, she stepped out into the street. It was cold and snowing lightly; scattered flakes whirled past the streetlamps in an eddying wind. The sidewalks were slippery where yesterday's wet snow had melted and frozen to a slick. Along the icy surface, fringes of fresh snow scudded in waves. She was forced to walk slowly, though her whole body tingled with the urgency of her errand, on alert because she had left her children alone. It was how she used to feel going out anywhere when Bobby was a baby and still nursing – knowing he wouldn't take a bottle, that if he woke hungry before she returned, he would scream and scream rather than accept a rubber nipple.

Was that where it had really started, Russ saying 'I'm superfluous around here anyway, I've never felt needed here,' Russ walking out on them, not even hanging around long enough to see Mikey's passage into the world? Holly had her-self grown up without a father, her own having died when she was a few months short of three. Perhaps, in becoming a mother, she hadn't known how to make room for one. It seemed very long ago now. The boys were eight and six. She was a single mother, competent, responsible, self-sufficient. She had a job that paid the bills and fed the three of them. She was a grownup. Anyone looking out the window as she passed tonight would have seen a tall, fair-haired woman in her early thirties, energetic of bearing, purposeful in her movements – a woman confident enough of her own impor-tance in the world to radiate authority, even though her coat (bought second-hand) was not of the latest cut, and her boots were of cheap vinyl instead of leather.

Regarding herself thus for a moment, as if from the out-side, Holly felt an uncharacteristic pang, half of self-consciousness, half of superstition, as though she tempted fate, feeling so secure in herself. In that split second's vulner-ability she stopped paying attention to her feet and they slid out from under her, sending her flying on the ice.

Holly was unhurt, but the contents of her bag – left unzipped in her haste to go and get back quickly – were scat-tered on the ground, and the change-purse compartment of her wallet had popped open, spilling coins. She swore under her breath, touching her hip and thigh which felt tender and would probably show bruises in the morning, while she crawled about retrieving items – hairbrush, Chapstick, hand cream, compact, gritty wet quarters and nickels. Then she rose, slung the bag over her shoulder, and resumed her way. Her hands, gloveless, were cold and wet from the snow, and she dried them on her coat as she walked.

The convenience store stayed open until eleven. From a distance it looked empty, though bright-lit; straining her eyes, she could not see the proprietor behind the counter. Perhaps he was in back, taking stock for the next day. She quickened her pace, hoping her watch was not slow.

As she came closer, she saw that the clock in the window said five to eleven, but the door only rattled against her tug; it was locked. She stood in front of it dismayed, blank for a moment. There was a 24-hour store about five blocks away, but she dared not leave the boys so long. About to turn and go, she reached out again as if in the hope that her first attempt had been a fluke, and rattled the locked door. A movement in back caught her eye. The proprietor appeared in the stockroom doorway; he recognized her, and waved 'just a moment.'

This proprietor was the younger of two brothers who had taken over the business from their father, the same year Mikey was born. He wasn't much older than Holly. Though she came into the store several times a week, and had been doing so all these years, she knew almost nothing about him; their exchanges were limited to friendly chit-chat, wry remarks about the news or weather. If she came in with the boys, he always slipped them each a red licorice stick, winking, as they left; they called him the Licorice Man.

As he opened to her now, she said gratefully, 'I was about to go. I'm so glad you're still here. Sorry to bother you at closing.'

'No problem.' One side of his mouth turned up in an odd, lopsided grin; his eyes crinkled. Once years ago – during the crazy years, as she thought of them now, the years after Russ left when she stumbled through her days with an infant and a toddler, both still in diapers – Holly had gone to a support group where the leader suggested they make a list of things that made them feel good, a list they could fall back on when the going got tough – things like bubble baths with candles and incense, favourite records, favourite foods. At the head of Holly's list, surprising her since she never thought about him, was 'That guy in the corner store's smile.' For he had a smile for everyone, this man, sunny and open, whatever the time of day or night – one of the world's transfiguring smiles – and she realized that going into the store was something she could count on to make her feel good every time: that no matter what her mood, she had to smile back at him, and in the smiling recover a piece of herself and become, at least for that moment, whole again. But then he disappeared for a few weeks, his brother taking over full time, and when he came back the smile was gone – his face was frozen and inert. A mysterious virus – he'd told her the name of it, she could never remember – had attacked the nerves in his face, completely paralysing one side of it and severely limiting movement in the other, so that he talked through the side of his mouth, his lips barely moving.

'They say I may get it back, I may not,' he told her, shrugging. 'It can take a long time.' He was matter-of-fact, without self-pity. For a long time only his eyes smiled; but gradually, over the months, one side of his mouth regained enough mobility to turn up slightly. 'You're getting your smile back,' Holly told him then, noticing; and his eyes lit up at her and crinkled as he replied, 'You think so? You see a difference? I hope you're right.' And it did seem, as time passed, that it came back more and more. Now she was so accustomed to the odd, asymmetrical smile that she could no longer visualize the old one, and almost imagined that he *had* got it back completely – that this was the same smile that had brightened her days when she inscribed it at the top of her list.

Holly paid for her milk and thanked him, smiling back through the glass as he locked up behind her and prepared to close the cash. The wind was gusting a little. Already the sidewalk was furred with fresh snow, concealing the patches of ice so that walking was more treacherous than ever. She picked her way carefully homeward, wishing she had worn a hat. Her ears were cold.

On the front stoop she felt in her purse for her keys and couldn't find them. She shifted the plastic bag of milk to the crook of her elbow, pulled the purse wide open with both hands and peered into it, rummaging. Then she remembered her spill on the ice. 'Of all the dumb things.' She set the milk down on the doorstep and descended again to the sidewalk.

As she did so, the wind died down and a startling, dream-like stillness fell upon the street. The snowflakes tumbling past the streetlamp nearest her seemed to draw her eyes upward into their luminous funnel; she thrust her hands into her pockets and gazed up, mesmerized, until she began to feel as though her feet had left the ground and she were being carried skyward. For a moment she lost any sense of what she was doing out there, on the street, at eleven o'clock at night, hatless and gloveless and with the children alone in the house. She saw how the lamplight sparkled on the newly fallen snow, picking out individual flakes like sequins and setting them coldly ablaze. The city was quiet, muffled by snow.

Under its spell she stood there remembering a childhood dream. She was outside on a night very much like this one, walking all by herself, and suddenly she realized that she had no idea where she was. None of the houses looked familiar; it was late, only a few lights burned in upstairs windows. She began to walk faster, frightened, recognizing that she was lost. She had no dime for a pay phone; she saw no store where she could stop and ask directions. No cars passed. The snow fell thickly, glittering on the ground, fountaining sparks as her feet kicked it along. Just as panic began to overtake her, she turned a corner and recognized where she was. It was a street in her grandmother's neighbourhood, a walk of maybe six blocks to her grandmother's house. She had only to walk ten minutes, and she would be there, knocking on the varnished wooden door of her grandmother's apartment, smelling the homely, familiar smell of accumulated cooking that lingered in the stairwell and hallway of that building she had known since infancy. In her relief the night became suddenly, staggeringly, beautiful. The sky seemed to glow; the snowflakes tumbled dreamily around her, and the streetlamps woke diamonds in the pure field of untouched white that stretched before her. In delight and gratitude she walked along in the feathery snow as if on air, making no sound, filled with peace at the beauty of the night and the nearness of safety. She felt no hurry, no urgency. She knew where she was going. She was nearly there.

A year ago November, when they buried her grandmother, Holly had remembered this same dream. Winter came early that year; the first snow was falling as they stood in the cemetery – she and her mother and Darren, Mom's boyfriend, and Bobby and Mikey huddled close together, clutching the folds of her coat. (Bobby amazed her later by saying, 'Mom, I really didn't feel like Nana Trehearne was in that box. I tried to believe it, but I couldn't. Because I kept thinking she was standing right behind us, telling us not to be sad.') That night the temperature dropped, freezing the ground so that the small accumulation did not melt, and in the weeks that followed, snow fell again and again, wrapping the city irrevocably in its cold enchantment. On one of those nights, still dazed with loss, returning with the boys from some school event or other, Holly had a sense of déjà vu as they stepped off the bus and started down their street in freshly fallen snow that sparkled before them. Her dream returned to her whole, then, startlingly vivid, as though she'd dreamed it the day before; and with it the beginnings of peace, like a promise of shelter, like the dream itself.

Now she broke her trance and retraced her steps to the spot where she had fallen; she bent, intent, swishing one boot back and forth in the light powder that had accumulated, until a jingling told her she had found what she was looking for. Blotting the icy keys clean and dry against the lining of her coat pocket, she turned back towards the house, stopping again by the streetlamp to gaze up into the whirling night. Lingering there, she did not at first see Mikey, who had waked and called, and now stood framed in the glass of the front door, blinking in the light of the hallway behind him.

Shivering in his nightshirt, puzzled but unalarmed, he stood gravely looking out upon his mother in the snow.

Accept My Story

MELANIE FELL OFF the fire escape during one of the times she was living with Paula. She broke her leg and both hips and did something to her spinal column, and when they discharged her from the hospital ten months later, she walked with two canes and a brace, and they told her she was lucky to be alive.

People who knew her history were more careful about what they told her; even behind her back they never came out and said it, but they had their suspicions about the accident. How, they asked themselves (and their glances asked each other) do you *fall off* a fire escape? And it wasn't as though she'd never threatened. But Melanie said it was an accident, she was watering some plants, she said, that she and Paula had hung up there to brighten the view out the kitchen windows, and she lost her balance. It could have been true.

It could have been true, and I have accepted it as true, because I think of Melanie as a truthful person. I imagine it this way: a Saturday morning in mid-May, very fine and bright, the leaves at different stages of opening, still greeny-gold and frilly, the air fragrant and pleasantly cool; sweater weather. On Saturdays Paula likes to sleep in till nine-thirty or ten and then to have a leisurely, festive breakfast; knowing this and wishing to please, Melanie – who moved in three weeks ago – has slipped out at nine and gone round to the pâtisserie for chocolate croissants; has selected two perfect oranges (rewrapping them tenderly in their tissue paper) from the specialty fruit stand next door, and has come in quietly, fed the cats, and put on coffee. She's setting things out on the table when Paula pads in, barefoot, holding closed a man's terry robe torn at the shoulder. With her frizzy straw-coloured hair standing out in odd peaks and her eyes still sleep-crinkled, she looks preoccupied and severe.

'You're up early, Mel,' she says. 'What did you get? Oh, chocolate rolls, terrific. What are these?' She touches one of the oranges swathed in purple tissue.

'Those are the most *wonderful*-looking oranges,' Melanie cries, and then, swooping to demonstrate, 'I had to unwrap at least two dozen of them before I picked these two – they were all so gorgeous – and I think the girl thought I was crazy. Look, Paula!' She unwraps one and holds up the vivid fruit, pointing to where the glossy peel is marbled with crimson. 'I've never seen these before, have you? They're from Italy. The girl says she only has them at this time of year, beginning around Easter. I couldn't *believe* the colour – especially in the sun...'

'Blood oranges,' says Paula. 'That's what we used to call them. Or passion oranges. They're flecked with red like that all through the insides, too.'

'*Blood* oranges,' Melanie repeats with a dubious giggle. 'But the reason I got them, when I saw them I thought of that line from the Wallace Stevens poem – "Late coffee and oranges in a sunny chair" – that's all I can remember of the poem, you know? but it sounded so delicious to me, coffee and oranges in the sun.'

Sun pours across the table now. It's really the saving grace of Paula's small kitchen in this St. Urbain Street apartment, that it gets the morning sun, for the tall windows don't look out on much. They give on an inner courtyard, facing identical windows across the way and a network of black iron fire escapes, accessible by a slatted platform below sill level. Last week, when the weather began to be nice, Paula bought some flats of begonias and impatiens from a stand in front of one of the grocers on The Main, and she and Melanie potted the plants individually and hung them at different levels on the fire escape.

'We could even eat outside,' Melanie says. 'We could take some big cushions out on the platform, and sit in the sun.'

'Not my sofa cushions,' Paula says sternly, and goes off to dress. When she comes back, the coffee-maker is hissing, the windows are open, and Melanie is out on the fire escape, watering the plants. 'Come see!' she calls, leaning over the rail to reach a hanging pot, 'the whosits are opening, not the ones with the furry leaves. The other ones. They're pink and white.' And those are the last words she says before she comes to, in the hospital, nearly a week later.

I imagine Paula, whom I never met, as being stoical, brusque-mannered, tough. Making a point of her independence. But at the same time, tacitly dependent on Melanie for certain things – for a kind of liveliness; maybe for a sense of purpose. Say when Paula was twenty-three, the age Melanie is now, she gave up a baby for adoption, something she never talks about. Say she loved the father, a jazz musician several years her senior, but he couldn't handle the idea of a child at that point in his life; say he left when she refused to terminate the pregnancy, say in the end she signed the papers for love of him, for need of him, and in the very doing discovered that she had to leave him. Say all this happened in the United States, maybe some-where in the midwest; and to pull her life together she fled to Canada, to Montreal, and found a job as secretary at the YWCA – where one night she found Melanie, a fifteen-year-old would-be runaway, hiding in the washroom.

It isn't hard to see how her apartment would soon become Melanie's home away from home, and later, when Melanie was working and could share the rent, how it would become her actual home on a few occasions, each lasting several months. In between, probably, there were boyfriends – Melanie's, Paula's.

The two of them have to laugh at the way events in their separate lives fall out, time and again, to make roommates of them. 'Paula, it's me. It's Melanie. Rick and I broke up. I can't afford this place alone. Can I stay with you till I find something cheaper?' Paula is always glad to have her, always says, 'Sure, why don't you just move in? It'll save us both money.' It is the third time – Paula has recently broken for good with a married man who went back to his wife one time too many; Melanie has just received, in a lump sum, a student loan to go to summer school and complete her high school leaving – that the accident happens.

'Accident.'

'Happens.'

It's funny how clearly I can see Paula, given I'm making her up, given that however I rack my brain, I can remember nothing that Melanie told me about her, except that she was older, had been married, kept cats. I see Paula: fair-skinned, hazel-eyed, curly-haired – I see her lean but wide-hipped, partial to western-style jeans worn with a belt, mannish shirts and hats, shirt-style dresses for work. She's without vanity, wears no makeup, but she is scrupulous about skin-care, treating her face each night with hot towels and a camomile astringent to open and close the pores. After doing this, her face looks splotchy and sensitive till bedtime; Melanie's olive skin is her envy.

I see her as Melanie sees her, at home, her guard down. She walks around barefoot; smokes, but not excessively; reads murder mysteries to unwind. She turns on the radio to hear the news or late-night jazz that she hums along with, making tortured jazz faces, as she catches up with neglected housework, or chops veggies for a spaghetti sauce she's cooking ahead, for company on the weekend, or for the freezer for a busy week to come. She has a TV but watches only the rare movie; she lets

Melanie keep the TV in her room. In her voice a faint midwestern twang still resides, and in her speech, certain midwestern idioms. She doesn't smile a whole lot. ('A whole lot' is something she would say.) She doesn't talk a whole lot either, and what she says comes out dry and lightly ironical, an habitual tone of hers, self-deprecating, unsentimental. Melanie is used to it; herself given to effusions, she simply effuses, oblivious. They make an odd counterpoint, the two of them, in conversation.

I can see the cats, too, a pair of Siamese females named Lily and Nessa, a mother and daughter. Nessa is a little larger and that's the only way Melanie can tell them apart, though Paula insists their personalities are quite distinct. Lily, as a kitten, was a gift from the married man during the early days of his courtship of Paula; Paula had her bred because it didn't seem fair to get her spayed before she'd had a litter. She sold the other kittens for what sounds to Melanie like a fortune, and kept Nessa; then shipped Lily off to the vet. Nessa wasn't granted the same grace; she was shipped off right after her first heat. '*Why?*' asks Melanie. 'You could've got *rich* doing that,' but Paula only shrugs, blowing smoke rings, and says, 'Too much hassle.'

In the years since she met Melanie, Paula has forged ahead. She's taken management courses at night, has gone from an administrative position at the 'Y' to a position as co-director of a local multicultural community project. She has learned French and spent a summer in Greece. Her loans are paid off, she's kept the apartment on St. Urbain because the rent is cheap, she's saving her money to buy a house. Melanie is wide-eyed at all of this. In the same period, she has been through several personal crises, three psychiatrists, a couple of love affairs (one of them with the second psychiatrist), four months as an in-patient, and more jobs than she can remember. She has gone from little pink pills to big white pills to amber capsules to no pills and back to little pink pills; from pills that made her feel stupid to pills that gave her tics and twitches, pills that made her hyperventilate and pills that closed up her throat during the night so that she'd wake choking. But Melanie has also audited university courses with the latest boyfriend, and has decided she wants to go to school 'for real' if she can just get her high school leaving. She wants to study English literature; for years she has written poetry that Paula thinks is 'darn good'.

Sometimes Paula knows, admits to herself, that Melanie is her child in a way, is a fast-forwarded version of the baby girl she relinquished – come to her by a miracle, returned to her so soon, already a woman, yet with an infant's fierce needs, a child's unconditional acceptance. But Paula is not given to this sort of thinking. If she feels an unreasoning anger when after a few months, on some whim, Melanie says she's moving out, Paula attributes it to Melanie's character: the girl is fickle and irresponsible. She doesn't need psychiatrists; she needs a good kick in the pants. Look at her, she's messy and undisciplined and plain lazy. So let her go. It will be nice to have the space again. And after a week or two during which the emptiness is so acute that Paula paces the floor at night, forgets to eat dinner, bites her nails to the quick – eventually it is.

I think of Melanie as a bit of an *enfant terrible*, but somehow invulnerable. In a way she's much tougher than Paula, though she is much more gullible, naive, overtly feminine. She has going for her that her own life and doings and what befalls her is intensely interesting and surprising; she has that detachment. It's her gift. She can always stand back from herself, her own life is like a very good novel, or the soaps. It never bores her. She is not at all inclined to self-pity or bitterness, does not bear grudges; she's generous in her interpretation of others. Paula still thinks she should go after the second psychiatrist, take the thing to court, he oughtn't to have been able to get away with that; but Melanie won't consider it: 'I couldn't do that to him,' she says, 'the poor guy. I mean, he has kids and everything. Do you think a man like that can help himself? I was just stupid.' She can seem a scatterbrain, but there's a saving intelligence underneath, that gets her out of scrapes just in time, or that allows her to forgive herself her errors, pick herself up, and move on.

Pick herself up. Did I say that?

But yes, that's how I've imagined it, imagined her. For really this Melanie, this adult Melanie, is as much an invention of mine as the Paula I've pulled out of the air, pulled together from fragments of other women I've known, bits of their stories. I scarcely knew the adult Melanie. I knew a child: my best friend in grades two and three, then an absent friend, when she moved with her parents to an outlying suburb in grade four. A voice on the telephone, almost nightly for a year or two (when we both still lived for rare weekend sleepovers), but less and less often over the years as we formed new friendships, became entrenched in our separate lives. Dimly, through the self-absorption of adolescence, I heard from my mother, who sometimes spoke to her mother, of Melanie's first breakdown. But it was unreal to me. Melanie, on the occasions when she phoned, still sounded like Melanie to me, and she was circumspect about her troubles, whatever they may have been. 'Did you hear?' she might ask, as if in passing. 'Did your mother tell you? No, but I mean, did she *tell* you? That I'm Seeing a Psychiatrist?' Sigh-*ky*-atrist, she pronounced it, with theatrical emphasis; then a stream of embarrassed giggles. What did I think, she'd want to know. Not knowing what to think, feeling I was being tested, I'd murmur something cautious, something I hoped was encouraging. More giggles. And then, perhaps, 'He's really cute. Do you believe me? My sigh-

ky-atrist, I mean. I see him twice a week. Tuesdays and Thursdays. He's a doll, no kidding!'

The week I started university was the week Melanie went into hospital. I remember that, because she phoned me – she phoned to wish me luck, wistful, vicariously excited – and I felt what a gulf had opened between us, how different our lives had become and were to be. I remember the constraint I felt during that conversation, the relief of putting the phone down. Melanie never asked me to visit her. I never thought of it. We hadn't seen each other for years, at that point, anyway.

Later there was a summer, part of a summer, when she roomed with me: she'd found a job downtown, near the university, and I had an apartment near there; one of my roommates was going to be away for a month and wanted to sublet her room to save money. I forget how it came about, whether Melanie phoned, or whether I ran into her, just at the moment when she was looking for a place and I was looking for a roommate. Anyway she moved in. I was a little nervous about it, but she got along well with the others – shared my room for the first two weeks till Jan left, then settled into Jan's – finding everything greatly to her liking and exuding an infectious, if slightly overwrought, enthusiasm for our ménage in all its details.

There were three of us on the lease, and when Jan came back, Melanie wanted to stay on – to sleep in an alcove by the entranceway that could be closed off with a curtain, and to pay a quarter of the rent. The others concurred, but four in the house sounded like more chaos than I could handle during the school year, so I argued against. No, be honest: it was Melanie herself, and what I knew of her past, that gave me pause; and though I didn't say it, the others sensed it and came hotly to her defence. There was some unpleasantness, and finally *I* moved out, to a bedsitter of my own, and Melanie took my room and signed the lease in my stead. I heard several months later that it had ended badly, with pots and pans flying and a fist-fight over rent owing. I felt vindicated.

And after that, I saw her only once, in maybe my second year of graduate school, something like that. She called, she'd got my number from my mother, she was going to be in the neighbourhood, could we have lunch? It was mid-April, term-paper season for me, but I figured I could take an hour off. We agreed to meet on a certain corner, near a restaurant we both knew and had frequented during the apartment summer.

'You may not recognize me,' she warned. 'I'm shorter than I used to be.'

'You're what?'

'*Well.*' The dubious giggle. 'I had an *accident*. But I'll tell you when I see you. I just thought I should warn you, so you won't be shocked.'

She was, in fact, about four inches shorter. She'd had some vertebrae removed, making her short-waisted. She was heavier, too. She came limping towards me on her canes and only the absolutely unabashed, unfeigned delight of her smile – a smile I could see from half a block away – got me through the awkwardness of our greeting. 'I fell,' she volunteered. 'Last spring. I fell off a fire escape. I just got out of the hospital a month ago.'

In the restaurant we ordered grilled cheese sandwiches and milkshakes, our old standard, and she told me a little more. She'd been living at her friend Paula's when it happened. Had she ever told me about Paula? She hadn't? That was funny, because she'd lived with Paula a couple times before. Paula was a divorcée – a lot older, but she was a really good friend. She was a character. She had (and now I remember it wasn't Siamese cats at all, it was dogs, little dogs) Pomeranians, had I ever seen a Pomeranian? Paula had two of them, they were 'just the most adorable things'. The limp was permanent. She'd had three operations. She would never walk without a cane.

Melanie amazed me that day, by her seeming equanimity at the prospect of living the rest of her life partly crippled, in her misshapen body; by her improbable cheerfulness. She surprised me, too, by apparently harbouring no hard feelings towards me, or anybody else, over the apartment episode: she asked after our former roommates in genuine interest, and had only nice things to say in remembering each of them. 'Jan's in *law* school? You're kidding! Gee, I liked that girl. She was so *original*!' Once or twice, in response to things I said, she let out a scream of laughter that made people at adjoining tables look over our way, and I felt a wave of embarrassment, a desire to escape. I remember trying to tone things down, asking her about her ten months in hospital, how could she have stood being in there so long? But this evoked the same scream of laughter. 'I loved it! The hospital was *wonderful*! I know it sounds crazy, but I had a wonderful time. Everybody there was so good to me, and they all said they liked me so much, and how brave I was, and everything. They made me feel so special! On the day I left they made a big party for me and everybody was crying. I never wanted to leave, Ruth, honest. I'm telling you, I could write a book about what it was like in that place, everybody that I met and all.'

Oh, Melanie. How easily I believed you, how badly I must have needed to. 'You should do that,' I said, getting up to put my coat on and fishing my change purse for a tip. 'You always wrote so well.' I was thinking of her grade-school compositions that the teacher always read out loud, and of the occasional poems and stories she'd shown me or read to me over the telephone, over the years.

'Gee,' said Melanie, also getting up – it seemed to take her a long time, and I wondered if I should help her, but felt awkward to offer. She managed by herself. 'Gee, do you really think so, Ruth? You think I could?'

'I really do.'

'Gee,' she repeated in a happy voice, as if turning it over. 'Maybe I will.'

Not long after this exchange, and not without trepidation, I married a fellow graduate student with whom I'd had a somewhat stormy but intense relationship for a couple of years, and moved with him back to his home town on the west coast, where we both soon found teaching positions. His was a tenure-track university post, in the history department; but mine was a one-year contract, with renewal contingent on my finishing my M.A., which I'd shelved. Anyway mine was short-lived, because our daughter was born a year after I was hired, and I got pregnant again while still on maternity leave and had another little girl fifteen months later. Murray and I held things together for a number of years, probably longer than we should have; we split up when the girls were five and six – both finally in school – and after a few months' separation I came back east with them to be nearer my parents, and by chance got a pretty good job in a theatre box office. I don't mean great pay, it's not; but good because the people are interesting, and I get free tickets to all the shows, and they lay me off in the summers so I can collect unemployment insurance and be home with the girls. Murray takes them for a week at Christmas and for three weeks in August – pays their plane fare – and he's been pretty good with the child support, I can't complain. It's not perfect but I really can't complain. Not compared to other women I've known.

During the whole time I was on the west coast, I wasn't in touch with Melanie. I spoke to her only once more – very shortly after my return. Again, it was she who called; again she'd got my number from my mother, who filled her in on where I'd been and what I'd been up to and why I was back. Melanie had some reason for phoning, something about wanting to enroll in university and thinking I'd be a good person to ask advice on which courses to take. She'd met someone, she told me; she was living with him, it had been a few years, but they weren't married. He was a salesman of some sort, he thought it would be good for her to do something with herself, because she got depressed when he was on the road. She hadn't been able to work since her accident, but she thought she could manage school.

At the time, I was too depressed myself to have much to say. It was nice to know that Melanie had found somebody, that she was looked after. It was also nice that she didn't ask anything about Murray. Actually, she'd met him – it was during the apartment summer that I'd begun seeing him – and in fact it was he who'd been behind my decision to move out of 'that cloister' as he called it, and away from 'those giddy schoolgirls'. Melanie did ask, wistfully, what my daughters looked like. She was thrilled that I'd had children; she never would be able to, now. (I remember being startled by that, I hadn't put it together. When we were kids, we used to talk about the children we were going to have when we grew up, we even had their names all picked out.) She hinted that she would love to see my girls, and I think I said something lame about maybe once I was more settled and had found a job. I wasn't up for seeing people much, those days, and Melanie, with her air of girlish expectancy and her willingness to admire me, was one person I knew I couldn't handle seeing at all – not right then. I took down her phone number, but on a piece of paper, not in my phone book; and subsequently I lost it. I never heard from her again.

Nor will I, because I found out last week that Melanie is dead. She died three and a half years ago, in early December – oddly enough, on the same day that the court heard my Declaration for Divorce. I know it was that day because I looked the date up, I wanted to place it somehow; ever since Caitlin was born, I've kept my old calendars. There it was, a Wednesday, circled, with 'Court hearing, 9:15 a.m.' written underneath. So I can picture the day exactly: it was heavily overcast, sombre; it hadn't snowed yet, because I remember I was wearing shoes, not boots, and walking down St. Antoine to the courthouse, my feet were cold. Murray was waiting just inside the main doors, smoking. He was on some sort of semester leave to do research for a book, so he'd been able to come east and co-file with me, saving lawyers' fees. He was staying with old school friends, and seeing the kids some – not as much as they'd expected, though, and not very reliably – and we weren't talking to each other much because at the last minute he'd stuck me with all the paperwork for the divorce (we were supposed to share it) saying he couldn't do that *and* see the girls and keep up with what he was supposed to be doing on his book. I was mad about that and about his cavalier scheduling of visits, based always on his convenience and subject to cancellation on short notice, leaving me to pick up the pieces. I remember on that day, the day of the hearing, he looked haggard and ill at ease; he had dark circles under his eyes and I noticed he also had deeply etched creases around them that were new, that I hadn't registered before. If he had even once looked at me directly, I might have felt compassion towards him, but he didn't, he made sure never to meet my eyes. There was a short wait in a crowded, smoky hallway where people were milling around a notice sheet to check their names on the list, and then we were called in.

The whole thing took all of about three minutes. I'd been prepared to defend our agreement if necessary, I had three typed pages of notes ready, but the judge never questioned us. Did we want to waive the thirty-day delay, he wanted to know. Taken by surprise, I glanced at Murray, who said, expressionless, that it was all right with him. So I said yes too. The judge declared us divorced, effective immediately, ordered us to respect the terms of our agreement, and we were ushered out before I'd had a chance to realize what had happened.

This was the 'new' divorce; do-it-yourself, short-order divorce. It was supposed to spare people a lot of the pain and expense and nastiness of the old divorce. Instead it left me feeling the strangest kind of emptiness, at once as though nothing at all had happened and as though I'd been robbed. What, was our whole marriage, our life together as parents of two children, our decision to end that, and the hard work of finding our footing apart, something to be dismissed in three minutes? Should we not have been required to stand up and account for ourselves, to plead 'Accept my story'? Weren't we entitled to have it acknowledged publicly that what we were doing was a serious thing? Or what were we doing there?

I didn't think any of this in so many words at the time – I just felt funny, unreal – left hanging, or as though I'd stepped out into empty air. We came down in the elevator silently, and at the door I asked Murray if he wanted to go get a cup of coffee somewhere, because it felt so abrupt the way it was, but he said in an abstracted voice, 'No, I think I'll pass.' So we shook hands on the street, a little formally (even then he wouldn't meet my eyes) and turned in our separate directions. I walked up to Ste. Catherine and along there to my bus stop, the sky was leaden and oppressive, Christmas decorations were up in all the store windows. I came home and felt (I'd asked for the day off, thinking we might have hours to wait, but I was home by ten-thirty) – I felt, the only word for it is 'nothing', I felt 'nothing', like a vacuum of feeling, all day. I remember the house was very dark, but I didn't feel like turning any lights on. I sort of folded myself into an armchair by the window and read – this is silly, but I read *Heidi*, because it was there, on the arm of the chair, Caitlin had it out of the school library. So I read *Heidi* – the whole thing.

At four-thirty, when the school bus was due, I walked out to the end of the next block to meet it where it stopped, and suggested to the girls that we go downtown to look at the store windows and then to a restaurant for an early dinner, pizza or Kentucky fried, whichever they preferred. It was a transparent move on my part. Caitlin asked right away, 'Did you go to court this morning with Daddy?' (had I really expected her to forget?) – and, when I said yes: 'Are you divorced now?'

I said yes again, in a voice that came out inadvertently squeaky, and then Bronwen, bursting into tears, cried, 'Well, I think that was a *stupid* idea!' and broke away from my reaching arms to run ahead. She ran all the way home; when we caught up to her she was on the porch, kicking savagely at the locked door, but she'd stopped crying. Later we went for Kentucky fried.

Sometime that afternoon, across town, Melanie left the apartment she shared with the salesman I never met, walked five blocks to a similar apartment building on the other side of the Expressway, entered the building, somehow gained access to the roof, and jumped.

I happen to be a rememberer of birthdays and anniversaries, of special dates; I'm a believer in the significance of dates. So the coincidence of dates, though odd, was no surprise to me – nor did it seem strange that it was on Melanie's birthday that I learned of her passing.

It was a coincidence and not a coincidence. The coincidence was the postcard that arrived that day from Murray's sister Nora in Vancouver, apologizing for not having answered my last two letters. The card explained she'd been too upset to write ever since Tom, a former lover who'd remained her dear friend, 'jumped out a window, taking his leave of us dramatically.'

I'd been close to Nora during the years Murray and I were together on the coast, and I stayed close to her after we separated, because Nora had been through a divorce herself and helped me out a lot during those first months, before I moved back east. We've corresponded since. Nora was the single soul who supported me in my decision – the decision to move back east – going against Murray and his parents and what all the pop-psychology books advised. 'Ruth,' I remember her saying to me as I anguished over it, 'Look after yourself first. Think about *you*, stop thinking about everyone else, forget other people. What I'm hearing from you is a lot of second-guessing, what's right for the children, Murray, Gram and Gramps, everyone but the cleaning lady. You need to do what's right for *you*, Ruth. You need to go down into yourself and listen to your deepest inner voice. Just keep going lower – Get into the elevator and hit the DOWN button. It'll stop on every floor, but keep going one lower.'

What *wasn't* a coincidence was that I'd been thinking of Melanie all day – it was her birthday, that's why; I'd had to write a cheque that morning, and as I dated it, my special-date bell went off: Ding! *Melanie's birthday.* So she was on my mind. It was on my mind to try and get in touch with her again. I'd tried before: there comes a time, in the wake of divorce, when one looks to reconnect with one's past, when one steps cautiously out onto the rotted planks of such bridges as remain. She wasn't in the phone book, or hadn't been last time I'd looked, and I didn't know the name of the man she was living with, assuming she was still with him. Her parents had long since gone separate ways and sold their house; they were neither of them listed. What had become of Melanie? Had she enrolled in university? Written her book? Had she had another breakdown? Was it strange that she'd never tried to call me again – or had she perhaps left town? Suddenly I wanted badly to speak to her, to hear her voice again. I thought of her ebullience, her generosity of spirit. I remembered her screech of laughter that was pure delight. I imagined getting her number somehow, dialling it, astonishing her by singing 'Happy Birthday' over the telephone – only, to give myself away, instead of 'Dear Melanie' I'd sing 'Dear Lemony,' her baby name for herself and a childhood joke of ours. There would be a moment of shocked silence – then she would cry, 'Is it Ruth? *No!* – is it *Ruth?*' – and I would hear that laugh. How nice it would be!

So she was on my mind when I got home from work and picked up my mail from the mat and read the postcard from Nora. And it was like – I can't say that I knew right then, that would be stretching it – but I knew there was something strange about getting that postcard on Melanie's birthday.

And later that evening, when I managed to connect (I remembered the name of a cousin of hers, I found him in the phone book, he was away on business but I spoke to his wife) – when I was told, hesitantly, that Melanie had passed away a couple of years back, she didn't want to say more, she'd have Hal phone me when he got home next week... I didn't have to wait for the phone call. I knew right away, I felt in my stomach, the way she'd gone. The same way as Nora's friend. She'd hit the DOWN button – her way.

Hal phoned last night. He didn't remember me, but he remembered who I was. He remembered some of the games he and Melanie and I used to play in the courtyard behind the apartment building where he and she both lived as children, before Melanie moved to the suburbs: he even remembered the names of some of the kids from the building opposite, who used to play with us. We talked for a long time. It felt strange to talk to this grown man, married and with children of his own, virtually a stranger, and to find in his memory bank things I too remembered and things I had not remembered, which now flashed vividly before me. As a teenager Melanie had had something of a crush on him. She saw him infrequently, at family holiday gatherings, and she used to phone me afterwards to report: 'Remember Harry, my cousin?' – he was Harry in those days – 'Well, I saw him on the weekend and he's three inches taller than I am. He's even shaving. And you know what? He's gotten really cute!' They used to talk on the phone; one summer they were at the same camp, and Melanie came home bemoaning the fact that first cousins weren't allowed to marry.

'I always stayed in touch with her,' Hal told me. 'We spoke to each other pretty regularly, every two-three months anyway, right up until the end. Apart from the funeral I only met her boyfriend once – they came to my wedding. He seemed like an okay guy, but he didn't like to socialize, and it was hard for her to get out and around on her own. So mostly it was phone calls.' He admitted it was usually Melanie who did the calling.

'You know, she always had her problems,' he went on. 'You must know that. I think she may have been manic-depressive, she was on pills, I don't know what exactly. But it went way back. Even at camp – she was always in the infirmary, she couldn't keep food down. They called it nerves. Why she did what she did – why at that moment – who can say? Apparently things were going all right, there wasn't any crisis, she was getting along fine with Stevie. She was even going to school – taking courses in English literature, I think, something like that. Getting A's. Figure it out. You know she'd tried before, though, you did know that, didn't you? In her early twenties.'

'I thought she had an accident,' I heard myself saying. 'She told me it was an accident. That she fell off a fire escape.'

'No, no. It wasn't an accident. It was the same thing – off a building – but only three storeys that time. She told you it was an accident?' And down tumbled my loving invention:

the sun streaming into the little kitchen, the flowerpots on the fire escape, the vivid vermilion of the oranges in their purple tissue. Paula; the cats. Had I ever really believed it?

Not an accident.

He filled me in briefly on the family, the funeral, Melanie's parents. In the background I could hear small children tussling and squalling; he interrupted himself a couple of times, 'Jonathan, put it down. I said PUT IT DOWN. Tracey, let go of his leg. Go brush your teeth – did you do pooh yet?' The third time, he laughed apologetically and said, 'Listen, things are sort of degenerating around here, my wife's out at a day care meeting. Can I give you my aunt's address, in case you want to write to her? You can call me any time if you want to talk more.'

I took down the address. 'Thanks, Hal.'

'Yeah, well, thanks too. I'm sorry. I appreciate your calling. It's nice to know she's remembered.'

As soon as I put the receiver down, Bronwen marched in. 'Are you off now? Rachel was supposed to *phone* me, we have to arrange stuff for tomorrow, *I* can't call *her* 'cause she's at her grandmother's and I don't have the number. How's she supposed to phone me if you're on the phone the whole night?'

'Don't whine. What's tomorrow?'

'Mom, I told you a million *times*, Rachel and Jessica and I have to get together to finish our geography project, it's due Monday, we have like *two days*!'

'Why'd you leave it so late, then?' Caitlin, in her prissiest voice. 'I'm sorry, but I'm calling Rosemary back, she phoned while we were eating dinner and I promised.'

'*Mom*! You can't let her!'

They're eleven and twelve now, in a year Caitlin will be the age Melanie was when she wanted to marry her cousin. She's going to camp for three weeks this summer; Bronwen went last. Even with Murray's contribution and help from parents, I can't afford to send them both in one year. I try to imagine Caitlin in the infirmary, throwing up, but I can't: Caitlin has a cast iron stomach. It's Bronwen I sometimes worry about, Bronwen who's high-strung, moody, who gets sent home from school with unexplained stomach pains or who wakes in the night with violent headaches – Bronwen for whom I leave work early or call in late, fuming over lost pay and unbudgeted taxi fares and three-hour waits in clinic waiting rooms to be told, 'She's okay, we can't find a thing.' Yet it's Caitlin whose teachers say, year after year, 'We worry about her sometimes, her work is lovely but she seems so rigid somehow, so very self-controlled, we never see her let go and just have fun like the other children.' I wonder what they used to say to Melanie's mother – the doctors, the teachers. I wonder what they didn't say.

September sunlight is streaming down through the tall schoolroom windows: long, slanted afternoon beams in which the dust motes circulate dreamily, just out of reach. It's the first day of second grade, five past three, time to go home. To our class has fallen the teacher everyone says is the best, the one everyone has had their fingers crossed to get: Miss Carsley, the pretty, smiling teacher everyone adores. In the schoolyard this morning they told us we were lucky ducks: 'You have Miss Carsley? Oh, you lucky duck!' But lovely Miss Carsley has just betrayed us, has stunned us, by saying she will keep the entire class after school until the person who whistled in the cloakroom 'owns up'. It's deathly quiet in the classroom. The bell has rung; the staggered footsteps of class after dismissed class have receded down the corridor; only we are left. We are sitting in our seats with our sweaters or jackets on and our schoolbags packed and our hands folded on our desks, waiting. And nobody owns up. The red hand on the big classroom clock jerks away the seconds. Somebody shuffles and fidgets, somebody else coughs. 'I can wait all night, if necessary,' says Miss Carsley, her lovely features unperturbed, seating herself at her own desk and beginning to sort through some papers, just as though we were no concern of hers at all. Oh! the wickedness; she can't really mean it! Our eyes are upon her, wide with dismay.

Maybe five minutes have passed this way, but it feels like hours. I have my hand raised, but Miss Carsley doesn't look up. Without my consent, humiliatingly, something like a sob escapes me; at this she responds. 'Yes, Ruth, what is the trouble?'

'My grandmother will worry if I'm late.' I relay this plea shakily. My grandmother is babysitting today. Once last year, when I dawdled after school to play in a puddle, she called the police.

Across the aisle and two seats down, a dark-haired girl in a yellow sweater has raised her hand too.

'I have to meet my mother,' she explains. 'It's to go shopping. If I'm late she'll think I forgot and went home!' At the end her voice breaks too; she sniffs back tears. There's an undercurrent of derisive snorting from the boys.

'That will stop now,' says Miss Carsley. 'It so happens that I *know* who whistled, but I'm waiting for him to say so himself. For every five minutes that he delays the class, he can stay an extra ten.'

The culprit capitulates. The rest of us are released. Standing on the corner, waiting for the crossing guard, I find myself next to the girl in the yellow sweater – the other girl who cried. We look at each other covertly; tentatively, we smile. Ordinarily aloof with new children, I feel bold with this girl who has revealed in herself a fragility equal to mine. I ask her name.

'Melanie,' she says shyly, and then, smiling, suddenly

eager to share: 'When I was little, I couldn't say it. I said Lemony. What's yours?'

We both hated cooked carrots, arithmetic, skipping-rope games. We both got carsick. We were both obedient with teachers, timid with storekeepers, judgemental of our peers. We were always in the most advanced reading group. At recess we seldom joined the other girls; we had our own games, they were more fun. They were continuing fantasies, sagas, in which we starred in various roles, seizing upon whatever we had recently read or learned, and whatever the season had to offer in the way of props and landscape: fallen leaves and candy wrappers through the windy days of fall; snow mountains in winter, in whose caves we mined and cached ice diamonds, and down whose slopes we rolled giant round snow cheeses; canals, and lakes with icebergs, and glaciers of slush, during spring melting.

Early on, she confided to me, 'I have a thing I do, I always wonder if everyone does it. I call it the She game. It's when I'm by myself, like walking home from school or something, or even when I'm at home, I'm always thinking the story of what I'm doing, and sometimes I even say it out loud, like: *She trudged wearily up the stairs*, or *She raced into her room and flung herself down on the bed*. Do you ever do that?' I did do that. I was astonished and pleased to learn that somebody else did. When we played together at recess, as it developed, we played a variant of the She game; we played the They game. We narrated our adventures in turn, generous with each other, acting it out as we went along. Eagerly taking each other's cues, we invented other lives, ones we lived in tandem with our real lives. When she moved away, a bleakness fell over the schoolyard, and recess dragged. I tried to continue the stories by myself, but it wasn't the same.

I can remember when my girls were little, waking early on

weekend mornings and hearing them in the next room, narrating an accompaniment to their own play. It was that same endlessly inventive give-and-take, like jazz improvisation – Caitlin taking the lead and Bronwen jumping in, elaborating, embellishing. How it would pick up energy like a kite taking off, how they'd begin to interrupt each other excitedly, 'No, Bronwen; Bronwen! listen to me; I have a better idea, it *wasn't* a camper van, it was a *covered wagon!*' 'Murray,' I'd whisper, gently joggling him awake, 'Murray. Listen!' And we would tune in briefly, smiling into each other's sleepy eyes, tickled by their urgent pitch, their earnest baby voices. Then we'd doze off again, fading luxuriously in and out of sleep for as long as the game lasted before somebody fell and hurt herself or somebody got hungry; or till one of them, tiring of the play, sabotaged it into a squabble, and the grown-up day began.

In those days I still thought Murray and I could make it work. I still thought that what we'd done together, what I'd persuaded him to do ('They married and moved to the West Coast and started a family') was a story we could both keep adding to comfortably, a story we could both go with to last our lives.

'Figure it out,' Hal said to me. Why she did what she did. Why at that moment. One needs to figure it out, one feels if one could figure it out, it might be more liveable with. So many holes, so many missing pieces. I'm looking back now, from a great distance, at those two little girls – not *my* two little girls (grown suddenly, bewilderingly, as tall as I am, borrowing my clothes without asking) – but the two who cried on the first day of second grade and became best friends. I see them picking their way along the top of a snow mountain, not the one in the schoolyard but the one the snowblower has blown onto the front lawn; it's January, nearly dark by four-thirty, house lights are shining out onto the snow. I see them suddenly sit down side by side on the highest ridge, in the snow pants they have been forced to wear to play outside (they won't wear them to school any more) – and, laughing, let go and slide to the bottom, they've slicked it with previous slides so it's giddily fast. I see them inside, later, dumping snow out of their boots; the storm cuffs of their jackets and pants are caked with snow, they peel them off inside out, leave them steaming on the radiator; around their wrists soon appear tender, puffy patches of red that ache and sting.

I see them in the spring, standing on the edge of an immense puddle in the schoolyard, looking down: the water is very still, a black mirror reflecting a still-bare tree, overhanging branches, beyond them a few clouds moving slowly across blue sky. 'Stand right here,' Melanie is saying, 'and I'll show you something strange. No, don't lean over, you have to stand where you don't see yourself – just the sky. And there can't be a wind, it won't work if there's ripples. Now – look at the branches and then look past them at the clouds. *Stare*, I mean. Don't blink. There – are you starting to feel it? Do you feel like you're going to fall *down* into the sky? Like it's pulling you in? Isn't that scary?' They both feel it; they teeter for balance, laughing, and grab for each other. What would it be like to fall *down* into the sky? The teacher has been reading *Alice in Wonderland* to the class; would it be like Alice falling down the rabbit-hole – falling and falling and falling, but slowly, with time to think and look around? Would you keep falling forever?

And I see them in the summer, at Belmont Park where Melanie's mother has taken them for Melanie's birthday; they're trying to figure out how it is that when you get to the top of the Ferris wheel, your seat isn't upside down; they can't figure it out but Melanie has been on the Ferris wheel before and promises that it isn't. 'You'll see, Ruth, it's the most fun. The best part is where you're right on top and it stops. And you can see everything far away, and everything on the ground is so tiny – everything looks *toy*. It's a little scary but not *very* scary. Like thinking it might get stuck there, and you couldn't get down. But when you look all around – well, you'll see – it's wonderful! You kind of wish things could just stay that way – the way it looks from up there.'

I see them at the top of the Ferris wheel, tiny, gesturing against the sky. They have cones of cotton candy, beautiful pink, that Melanie says are like eating air.

If you were to say that as a child she had an attraction to the idea of heights, to the idea of falling – would you have explained anything? If you remembered that she had a terror of the skylight shaft off the bathroom of the apartment where she lived when you first knew her would it be a clue? Does it mean more to say a word like *manic-depressive*? To ask if there had been a crisis, if there had been a quarrel?

'Ruth,' I hear her saying, we're standing outside her door on the fourth-floor landing, we're seven years old, 'Do you know what a skylight is? Because there's a skylight in my bathroom.'

It's the first time I've been to her house. I don't know what a skylight is, I live in a duplex. Melanie's building is a squat, ugly five-storey apartment house, dun-coloured brick – one of so many identical post-war buildings, both sides and the length of her block, that it takes months before I recognize which is hers as we approach it. Melanie has made her announcement as if she were saying, 'There's a monster in my bathroom,' and now she asks, worriedly, 'Will you be afraid to use the bathroom?' She's hoping I can sleep over.

The skylight, I soon see, is just a narrow shaft the window gives on, a dim brick well down which faint daylight filters, yellowish, through dirty panes. Windows give on it on all four sides. Across from Melanie's, someone has put a plant out on the sill. 'What's at the bottom?' I ask.

Melanie shrugs. She's standing in the doorway, watching me. 'You can look if you stand up on the toilet seat and lean your head against the screen. I looked once. It was just some old mops and brooms. I don't know why it scares me. My mother made me look so I'd stop being scared, but I still am. I never close the door when I'm in there.'

Irrational fear? Presentiment? Figure it out. Caitlin, at eighteen months, howled in terror at the sight of an umbrella opening. Later she was afraid of man-holes, escalators, oil-truck hoses. Bronwen still won't go down to the basement alone. I can't fall asleep if my closet door is open. Still, in the light of what I know now, the memory is startling.

What in us cries out for an explanation? Why can I not just say, 'My childhood friend grew up to suffer from a mental illness that led to her suicide in her mid-thirties'? For surely that is the essence of what happened to Melanie – as much as is given us to grasp. What is it exactly that one wants explained? The act? The timing? The method? 'Why her?' The implications for oneself?

All of it, bewildering – impossible to accept – too painful to think about. I jump away from it – as I must have jumped away from my own suspicions, other people's intimations, about the 'accident'. No, no, it couldn't have been that; I believed Melanie. I preferred to believe what Melanie told me, to accept her story. More than that: to re-create it from the cues she gave me – to embellish it, add on to it, *make* it be real. Did I invent Paula to be for Melanie what I knew inside I had not been? Someone whose door was open to her, who didn't back away. Someone who needed her.

After the girls fell asleep last night, I went downstairs – I went down to the basement and for the second time this week, opened the old steamer trunk under the stairs. The trunk is an antique; I bought it in a junk shop in Victoria, as a pretty thing to store linens in, and used it to ship the shards of my life back east in when I split with Murray. Once here, I unpacked what was useful and banged the lid down on everything else, all the old pictures and papers and memorabilia that had crossed the continent with me, some of it twice. Things that had become obsolete, like my half-written master's thesis and the notes for it, maternity clothes, baby clothes – and things I couldn't bear to look at, like wedding pictures and baby pictures and family snaps. After we were legally divorced, I sifted through most of it again and threw out a lot of stuff, had a few of the old pictures framed, pulled out some odds and ends that had decorative or sentimental value, and repacked what was left. Since then I seldom lift the lid, except at the end of each December when my used-up calendar gets added to the pile, and whatever letters I've kept over the year are filed away.

When I opened it last night, the calendar from the year Melanie died was on top, where I left it last week. That wasn't what I was after; I wanted to see if among my childhood relics buried at the bottom, there wasn't a picture, a letter, a keepsake – some concrete reminder of my friend. In a brown envelope labelled 'Grade School' I found our third-grade class picture, but to my disappointment Melanie wasn't in it; she must have been absent the day it was taken. I dug around for a while thinking there might be something else, maybe a snapshot of us at Belmont Park or at some other birthday celebration, maybe an autograph book, a card ... but there was nothing. And then, as usually happens when I dip into the trunk, I sat leaning against its ribbed side on the cool basement floor for a long time, diverted by what I'd pulled out to get at what I was looking for – poking into things and reading things before

I put them back. I found a packet of old letters Murray wrote me from the coast during the summer we were apart, a year after we met. It was strange to read them again (I'd forgotten they existed) and to see, in retrospect, how clear it was from their tone – coolly intellectual, controlled, enjoying their own cleverness – that he was not much in love with me, that these were not love letters. Yet I remember receiving them, I remember tearing them open sitting on the front stairs of the rooming-house where I then lived, and reading love into them, because it was what I'd decided was happening, because it was what I wanted.

The thing I wish I'd kept to remember Melanie by – and it was something I did keep for a long time, I still had it knocking around my room when I was in high school – was a cut-glass doorknob that Melanie spotted on the way home from school with me one day, in a rubble heap from a building where there had been a fire. This became for the two of us something of a sacred object, central to much of our play, where it figured at one time as a fabulous jewel we had to protect against thieves or recover from thieves, at another as a talisman of magical powers, but oftenest as a divining crystal, a crystal ball. We took turns keeping it in our houses; I forget how it ended up with me – probably that's just where it happened to be when Melanie moved. Its facets caught and flashed the light, reflecting distortions of nearby objects, and we liked to gaze into it and describe to each other the worlds we saw inside, imagining ways we could make ourselves small and enter them. That was an idea Melanie came back and back to; when our teacher finished *Alice in Wonderland* and followed it with *Through the Looking Glass*, she was enthralled – 'Ruth,' she used to say, 'don't you love the part where the mirror begins to get hazy and she climbs through, into a different world? Don't you wish we could do that? Sometimes when I'm alone in the house I stand in front of the big mirror in the hall and stare and stare at it, and just *wish* it would happen. And once I thought it *was* getting hazy, but it was just my eyes, from staring.'

It was well after midnight when I came back upstairs, checking on the girls before turning in as I always do. It's warm these nights; their window was open and the curtain was bellying in the breeze, lilac fragrance wafting in. An invisible line divides their room down the center, Caitlin's side austerely tidy, Bronwen's looking as though a hurricane struck it; Bronwen's bed is closest to the door, and I caught my foot in a loop of her schoolbag strap, going in.

I like to look at them asleep; the years seem to drain from their faces and I see the pure lines of their features as I remember them from infancy. Caitlin's head was thrown back, hands clasped behind it, mouth open; her fine light hair was beginning to unravel from the elegant French braid her friend Rosemary did up for her earlier this week. Bronwen lay on her stomach, arms around the pillow as though she'd fallen asleep tackling it. Her forehead was jammed against Digory, a plush dog she's had since she was five or six and still sleeps with, unabashed. Caitlin used to have a bedful of stuffed animals, but retired them to the closet a couple of years ago; Bronwen, whose fierce loyalty to Digory has precluded any other stuffed toy's joining him by her pillow, shows no sign of following suit; it was a foregone conclusion that he'd go to camp with her last summer.

I moved Digory away a few inches and lifted the hair from Bronwen's forehead, which was damp beneath my hand. She stirred in her sleep, a childish, sensuous movement, and renewed her hold on the pillow; she sighed. Digory slid to the floor and as I bent to retrieve him, I remembered another stuffed dog, I remembered the sad true story of Jackadandy, as told to me in the schoolyard by Melanie, not long after we first became friends. Jackadandy was her oldest toy, she'd had him from when she was still a baby; he was greyish and threadbare from going through the wash, and his legs had gone floppy so he couldn't stand up any more, but he was still her Jackadandy. By a terrible mistake, Jackadandy had got thrown out with the garbage one day. Melanie had been play-ing Space Dog with him, she'd made him a space suit out of a brown paper bag, and stuck him in her wastebasket for a Sputnik capsule, and had forgotten and left him there. When she remembered, she found that her wastebasket had been emptied that morning. Her mother hadn't looked, she thought it was just an old lunch bag in there. And the big gar-bage had been emptied too, because it was garbage day.

'We ran outside right away,' Melanie said. 'We went around the side of the building where all the garbage is put out, but we were too late – the garbage truck had already been. So I asked my mother where the garbage trucks take the garbage – where does the garbage go? And she told me it goes down the river. So now,' she concluded earnestly, touching my arm, 'when I think of Jackadandy, I just tell myself, 'Jackadandy went down the river.' And that way, I can imag-ine all the adventures he must be having.' She paused, she searched my face, did I understand? 'Instead of feeling sad.'

I guess it was something of the sort that I was casting for, down in the basement, when I sat on the floor with the letters in my lap and the picture in my hand, wishing that I'd kept the doorknob. It was crazy, but I guess I thought that if only I had the doorknob, the crystal doorknob – maybe I could look inside it and see Melanie, restored to wholeness, safely passed through.

(In Memoriam, E. M. S.)

The Paper Knife

A COUPLE OF YEARS into their friendship, in a mood of slightly giddy expansiveness probably brought on by cheap wine, Kayla told Toni, 'The first thing I ever heard about Ned before I met him was that he was a genius, and the first thing I ever heard about you was that you had big boobs.'

Kayla seemed to find this wonderfully funny, and to expect Toni to as well. She explained: 'I liked that, you know? I mean, it sounded like a match made in heaven. I felt happy for Ned. Isn't that really what a genius needs?' She laughed.

This was in the early seventies, when hip women went bra-less, or casually whipped off their tops to sunbathe, exposing little round breasts that stood up. Toni, who at twenty-two was still painfully self-conscious about her chest size, somehow managed to smile, covering her discomfiture at the revelation that Kayla had heard anything about her before they'd met – before Ned, who was renting Kayla and Dieter's back room at the time, first brought her over to the flat. It wasn't hard for her to guess that the source on both counts must have been Dieter, whom she'd met a few times on the street with Ned before she visited his room. Lanky, dirty-blond Dieter with his ink-stained fingers, his ice-blue stare and twitchy sardonic smile.

By the time this conversation took place, Toni and Ned were married, and Kayla and Dieter happened to be together again, though this was, as usual, not to last long. Toni and Kayla had become friends only after Kayla and Dieter first separated, when Kayla moved out of the flat and rented a room for herself in a converted Victorian mansion about three blocks away. Before that, they'd been acquaintances only. Toni was shy, Kayla was older and married, and when they were all together the men did most of the talking. The truth was they were not together much, because Ned, no doubt aware of tensions, was keeping a low profile in the house and doing his best to avoid the common kitchen when Kayla and Dieter were there.

Toni misread this at the time, and thought it betrayed that Ned felt she wasn't good enough for his friends: that to allow much mingling was to risk their finding her out. As what? As a third-year honours student with a 90 per cent average, living on scholarship money in a bourgeois high-rise apartment with a roommate who read *Vogue* – when everybody who was anybody had dropped out of university or flunked out or was taking time out to travel. As someone who'd never hitch-hiked to the west coast or dropped acid or been broke. It was true that Ned, who was broke a lot and owed Dieter three months' rent, was still in school – she'd met him there – but he meant just to finish his year and not go back – not *graduate*. He was only there for the connections.

Dieter had quit graduate school and was writing a novel called *Horse of a Different Colour*, when he wasn't sweating in the stockroom of Kayla's father's shoe store. Ned was at work on a full-length play, his first one-act having won a prize and been produced, to some acclaim, by the University Players. Kayla, who had once embarked on a qualifying year and dropped out after her first week of classes, was as far as Toni could make out doing nothing at all. She went for walks, she came home with bags full of clothes from the second-hand stores, she puttered about the kitchen making soups from dubious ingredients and regaling whoever was there with her own brand of fey, whimsical conversation that seemed to enclose the participants in a cocoon of intimacy. She was a tiny woman, with masses of black ringlets and eyes of a startlingly pale green that had a disconcerting way of fixing suddenly on something you couldn't see. She wasn't pretty in any conventional sense – her features were somehow oddly spaced – but it was a face you had to look at again. She looked as if she could be anywhere from thirteen to thirty; she was, in fact, twenty-two.

'I found her on the street,' Dieter would explain to anyone new, and right in front of her. 'I said, Come home with me now and I'll look after you, and she followed me home like a shy horse and spent the night, and that was it – I haven't looked back. I made a deal with her father, I make sure there's food on the table. Before, she was living like an animal.'

'And now?' Kayla might retort, mildly, when she bothered to respond, waving a hand at the paint flaking off the leaky ceiling pipes, the plaster crumbling out of holes in the wall where Dieter's fist or boot had left a dent during one of his fabled rages. She didn't have to say more than this to win a laugh from the assembled regulars, and a conceding, twitchy grin from Dieter. It was generally understood among them, Ned gave Toni to know, that Kayla had more brains and talent than any of them, that if she wanted to, she could do anything she chose to and go right to the top. She could sing, she could paint, she could act and dance, she was brilliant about literature in her no-bullshit way. This, in spite of an appalling childhood: her mother, incurably schizophrenic, had been committed to an institution a decade earlier; the grandmother who held things together died soon after.

People talked about Kayla in hushed tones; it was clear that not a few of the men (and some of their girlfriends too) were a little in love with her – Ned among them. Privately, he was indignant at Dieter's treatment of her – the public dressings-down over grocery money spent on flowers and incense or given to derelicts; the theatrical railings about late or burnt suppers, unwashed dishes, silk shirts thrown in with the regular washing, garbage breeding maggots under the sink. 'She's a genius, an absolutely rare being,' Ned would say, 'and what he wants is a suburban housewife. It sickens me.'

Covertly, Toni watched Kayla for signs of genius. She saw nothing conclusive. Kayla might sing, with a refreshing lack of self-consciousness, it was true, while mashing potatoes or carrying out the garbage, but it sounded to Toni like ordinary singing, a pretty voice, nothing electrifying. Of her painting, there was nothing to go on but the mural on the far wall of the kitchen, a collective effort in acrylics done, according to Ned, one legendary night when some cousins of Dieter's blew in from Europe and everyone was blasted on weed. Kayla's contribution of a fire-breathing dragon uncurling from a lopsided chimney had a certain charm, but you couldn't say it stood out from everybody else's.

'Do you paint a lot?' Toni once asked her, to make conversation while waiting over a pot of lukewarm tea for Ned to get out of the bath. She always felt awkward to find herself alone in the kitchen with Kayla, as if, unless Ned were beside her, she had no business being in the house at all. Kayla, who was stirring something on the stove, arms raised awkwardly to keep the sleeves of her caftan out of the pot, turned and peered at her vaguely. 'Do I *paint* a lot?' She sounded as though it required thought. Then she laughed cryptically. 'No. Why, do you?' Toni said quickly, 'No, I just wondered,' and felt acutely embarrassed, for having asked to begin with and for not knowing how to interpret the answer. She was prepared to believe that Kayla was a genius, to accept it on faith, just as she had come to accept that it was some fundamental lack of imagination on her own part that enabled her to tolerate classes in Honours English and hand in term papers on time, and to continue to accept the scholarship money that made it possible for her to live on her own in a real city, instead of attending the college of her home town and living with her parents.

[60]

That Dieter was a genius went without saying; and Franz, who rented the small double parlour as a studio and really did paint a lot, was certainly a genius; and among the house regulars were actors and musicians who were geniuses too. Toni wasn't a genius. No one who stuck university could be a genius. She'd caught Ned's attention, though, debating a point with the prof in their Elizabethan drama seminar; she was incisive, Ned said, she saw to the heart of things, and more than that, she was 'just astonishingly lucid'. He had a script he was working on; he wanted to show it to her. Toni clung to this.

By fall of the following year, she'd moved out of the high-rise into a furnished room of her own, a gabled one at the top of a decaying brownstone nobody could call bourgeois; and Ned, who'd gone back to school after all, was spending almost as much time there as he was at the flat, partly because he felt bad about the rent he owed, and partly to avoid what he called 'scenes' that were becoming more and more frequent. It was here that Kayla knocked one spring day, the day that what Toni thought of as their friendship really began.

Toni was surprised to see her. She hadn't even thought Kayla knew where she lived.

'Ned isn't here,' she said apologetically, her hand still on the doorknob. 'He spent the last few nights here, but he had an exam to write this morning and I figure he'll probably head home to your place afterwards.'

Kayla seemed to hesitate, but only for a second. 'So?' she said brightly. There was something almost coquettish in her voice. 'Does Ned always have to be around? I came to see *you!*' She was dressed strangely, even for Kayla. She was wearing lime-green stockings, yellow cloth shoes, a floral print skirt with a crooked hem that looked like it had come out of somebody's grandmother's trunk, and a hooded cape of burgundy velvet.

'Do you like my cape? I found it at the Goodwill. Do I look like Little Red Riding Hood? Can I come in?' She came in. She walked around exclaiming over the gabled windows, the two alcoves that nested the double bed and an old-fashioned writing desk, the round bevelled mirror, the cherry-wood wardrobe – 'It's cherry, isn't it?' – she stuck her head inside and sniffed deeply, and Toni felt something, a quick thrill of sympathy, that took her by surprise. 'It's a *beautiful* room, Toni! Do you pay a lot for it? I love to see where people live. So this is Toni's room.'

'But look at this,' Toni said impulsively, a little shyly, and she ran to the round mirror and lifted it off its nail on the wall for a moment. Underneath was a circle of dull green, startling against the soft rose colour of the wall. 'Can you believe this? Whoever lived here before painted without taking down the mirror – just painted around it!' They both began to giggle. Then, abruptly, Kayla plopped down on the bed. She opened her big cloth carry-all, dumped some of its contents and fished out cigarettes and matches. 'Toni, do you smoke? Do you mind if I do? Can I use this for an ash tray?' – picking up a polished abalone shell from the windowsill, a gift from Toni's brother. 'Toni, I have to tell you something. Dieter and I aren't living together any more. We broke up three days ago. He told me he didn't know why we were together any more, he can't write with me around, I make him crazy. At first I felt terrible, but then I thought, No, he's right. I'm the wrong horse for him, I'm too wild. You know that's what he calls me – Little Horse?' She began replacing the scattered items in her bag. 'Anyway, so I left, right away. I went to see this guy Matthew who I know, who inherited a lot of money when he turned twenty-one, and I asked him if I could borrow some money. I found a room pretty cheap, it's just around the corner, it's paid, for two months. Will you come see it? Can I make you some tea in my new place?'

Walking in the street beside Kayla, Toni felt something again, something she couldn't have named, unasked-for, a kind of grace. Kayla in her red cape and gypsy clothes seemed to give off rays of colour, to make a rainbow bubble in which the two of them floated like carnival queens. People looked twice at Kayla, people stared, and Kayla, smiling, waved and called 'Hi!' to them all, strangers though they were; and strangers though they were, they smiled too – huge, delighted, childlike smiles – and called back, 'Well, hi there!'

Kayla's room was at the back of the house, up a long narrow flight of stairs – 'The old servants' quarters, I guess. It's a bit of a mess right now,' Kayla said apologetically as she fumbled with the key. The tall, heavy door swung open into a dimness that smelled of incense and overripe fruit. The shade was still down; clothes were scattered about the floor. On a chair by the unmade bed, two apple cores and a bunch of brownish bananas flanked a full ash tray. Kayla touched a cord and the blind flew up with a snap, the light revealing faded wall-to-wall carpeting in a swirly pattern of pinks and grays. In the center of the room was an enormous potted plant, a kind of tree, with overgrown untrained upper branches arching stiffly down towards the floor, and clumps of dusty, yellowing leaves. All around it, on the carpet, were piles of powder-dry, spent potting soil; an open bag of fresh loam, spilling out blacker dirt, lay beside it.

'The landlady was going to throw this out,' Kayla explained, 'because she says it's dying. Well, no wonder, look what she had it in. Can you imagine, throwing something out because it's dying? I'm sure I can save it, I repotted it yesterday, only I don't have a broom or dustpan yet so I couldn't clean up. – Hi, animal!' She gave the broad upper leaves of the unruly plant a friendly flick. 'My, you're dusty. I'll wash your faces later, I promise.' She opened a drawer in the dresser and took out a small teak-wood chest, the lid inset with brass elephants – a gift box of loose Darjeeling tea. 'Matthew gave me this. Come,' she said to Toni, 'the kitchen's down the hall. I share it with the next room – such a funny man, a Communist, he has the reddest beard you ever saw and hair that sticks straight up. The day I moved in, I had no dishes or anything here – I still don't have much – so I used his, and I drank half a bottle of orange juice that he had in the fridge because I was really thirsty – and he made a big fuss. So I said, Who's the real Communist around here? I told him he could use anything of mine, any time. I think we're friends now, sort of.'

Toni liked the kitchen, which was spacious, with waxed green linoleum on the floor, and wainscoting, painted white. Sun slanted in through the French windows. Kayla boiled water in a saucepan – the gas flame made soft popping sounds – and brewed the tea, tossing in a cinnamon stick for fragrance; they sat at a white enamel table and sipped it from plain blue mugs they took from the dish drainer.

'It's nice here,' Toni said. 'It reminds me of – my grandmother had a kitchen sort of like this, when I was a kid.'

'So did mine,' said Kayla, and then, for no reason at all, they giggled again as they had when Toni moved the mirror.

In later years, Toni could never remember whether it was at the end of this first visit, or a subsequent one, soon after, that Kayla gave her the paper knife. Anyway it was early on – it was when they were only beginning to know each other. Toni was standing in the doorway of Kayla's room, saying goodbye, when Kayla stepped forward suddenly, catching her by surprise so that she momentarily lost her footing, and hugged her hard.

'I like you,' said Kayla, holding Toni by both hands and gazing up seriously into her face. 'I didn't realize – I mean, you're not at all the way I used to think. I like you a lot. And

I'm happy you're with Ned. Ned's a great guy, you know, really a special person. Wait, don't go yet. I want to give you something.' She turned around and undid the drawstring on her big cloth bag, it was hanging on the inside doorknob; she rummaged for a long time, seeming to consider and reject several possibilities. But then she drew out an exquisite little Chinese paper knife, curved like a scimitar, in a hand-painted enamel sheath.

'Do you like this, Toni?' she asked. 'It's a letter-opener. I found it in Chinatown last week, it cost more than I had with me, but I liked it so much that the man in the gift shop let me have it anyway – such a nice man, his name is Victor, Victor Fong. Oh! I'd love to walk all over Chinatown with you, Toni – look in the shops and then have tea and fortune cookies!'

On the knife sheath, a minuscule brown horse grazed under a minuscule blossoming tree, by moonlight.

'It's beautiful,' Toni said hesitantly.

'Good, then I want you to have it. I want to give it to you. Please. It's for you and Ned, for the two of you.' Ceremonially, she pressed it into Toni's hand. 'I'm so happy you like it.' And again, she hugged Toni hard.

'That must mean she's really taken to you, Kid,' said Ned, when she showed it to him later that day. In the sunny desk alcove of her room, where he had installed himself to work on a new play, he held the little knife and turned it over in his hands admiringly; the enamelled metal flashed, jewel-like, as it turned. 'What a magical thing! Kayla's someone who makes almost an art of giving gifts. She chooses her moment, she celebrates something – not a formal occasion, but something that she sees in another person. You've been given your moment, I see.'

'It's for both of us,' Toni protested, secretly warm with pleasure at his words. 'She said so.'

'Well then, a blessing of sorts has been conferred on us.'
And he handed her back the knife, smiling.

Why did it seem as though it was Kayla's stamp of approval
that finally clinched, for Ned, what had been nebulous –
unspoken and unbroachable – before? A week later, he asked
Toni to marry him; by September they were married.

2

Kayla didn't exactly break down your door with her visits.
She'd show up, now and then, and it was always as though no
time at all had elapsed, though in fact if you thought about it,
you might realize you hadn't seen her for weeks. She was
back with Dieter or she'd left him again; she was waitressing;
she was working in an art gallery; she was staying in an
ashram; she was living with her father; her father had
disowned her. She came with flowers; she came with exotic
fruit – pomegranates, fresh dates, mangoes; she came with
tales of strange encounters and strange characters, narrow
escapes and twists of fate; and for Toni she never stayed long
enough, for never did Toni laugh so much, or feel so
showered with blessings, as when Kayla sat at their kitchen
table, doodling wonders on a paper napkin or impersonating a
landlady or describing (as only Kayla could) a street scene or
the bizarre landscape of a dream. But for Kayla there was
always someone waiting, someone she'd arranged to see,
somewhere she had to be – and Toni soon learned that even if
Kayla promised to come back the next day or to meet someplace for tea, she would turn up late if she turned up at all,
full of apologies, having been waylaid by someone on the way,
or having remembered that she'd promised to do something
with somebody else, she could only stay a minute, could she
call you next week...? And you'd forgive her instantly; you'd
return her hug and watch her skip off down the street,

singing. *Dust be diamonds, water be wine; happy happy happy all the time, time...*

One cloudy afternoon in March, the spring after they were married (Toni was doing graduate work and had a teaching assistantship; Ned, having failed his final year for cutting classes, had quit at last and thrown in his lot with a foundering theatre company) Toni came home from class and, climbing the stairs to their apartment, caught a whiff of a familiar, fruity perfume Kayla was fond of. She turned the key in the lock with a quickened energy, calling, 'Kayla? Is Kayla here?'

'She was here earlier,' Ned answered from the living-room that doubled as a study for both of them. 'How did you know?' There was something hedgy, reluctant, in his voice. Toni was about to reply as she came to the doorway, but she stopped. Her eyes had come to rest, as though drawn, on an unfamiliar object on the mantelpiece – a box of polished ebony, on carved legs, intricately inlaid with what looked like mother-of-pearl. It seemed to be glowing. Without speaking, Toni moved towards it; afterwards, in memory, it seemed as if this happened in a dreamlike slow motion, in total silence – a sudden, frightening absence of sound, as in a Bergman movie. And it was as if she knew without looking that Ned was watching her, uneasily, passively, from the armchair in the corner.

'Where did this come from?' she asked strangely, her voice echoing slightly in the uncarpeted, high-ceilinged room.

Ned said nothing as she reached out and lifted the lid of the box. A Russian folk song, nostalgic and sentimental, began to tinkle. Toni stared blankly at four fat spools of coloured thread against a lining of red velvet, and shut the lid again, silencing the music that for no reason she could explain, then or afterwards, stirred in her a terrible sense of apprehension, of foreboding. 'Where did this box come from?' she cried, unable to conceal her agitation. 'Ned. Did Kayla give us this? Why did you let her?'

'Don't you like it?' Ned asked dully. 'She thought that you would like it.'

'But it looks very old. It must have been horribly expensive, if it's not an heirloom or something. Ned, you've got to give it back to her! We *can't* accept this, it's, it's... Ned! I don't want it.' She knew her distress was freakish, inappropriate; she could not account for it. The ebony box gleamed at her like something dangerous, like a Pandora's box that has come to stay.

'I don't see why we can't,' said Ned, but he wouldn't look at her. 'She very much wants for us to have it.'

'Just out of the blue?' cried Toni. They hadn't seen Kayla in over a month.

'Well, no, not exactly.' And then Ned admitted, still in that dead voice, 'It was partly in exchange for something.'

Toni felt cold. She didn't know how she knew, but she knew at once, before he said it, that he meant the paper knife, that the paper knife was gone. She said nothing. Ned went on, as if he too knew, without being told, that she'd guessed: 'Toni, she came to the door with it, she was distraught, she begged me to let her have the letter-opener back, in exchange. She's been seeing Dieter again, he gave her a silver bracelet and she wanted to give him something special in return – she had her heart set on its being a letter-knife like the one she gave us, because of the little horse on it – you know – because of his thing about horses. She said she'd been all over town trying to find another like it. Toni – what could I do? She was practically down on her knees asking me for it.' Now he faced her suddenly, unhappily, his grey-blue eyes flinging a troubled challenge. 'I know you cherished that little knife. I know. I just couldn't say no. If you'd been here ... I could tell she felt terrible asking for it – and I felt it would have destroyed her if I'd refused. She offered the box in exchange because she said it was the nicest thing she had, and she thought you would like it. It belonged to her grandmother, I think.'

'Oh, *no*,' Toni said quietly.

'What could I have done? She was so insistent that I take it, she was so grateful. Would *you* have refused her? Toni, please. Don't make her feel worse about this, don't mention it to her. Toni? Let it go. Please.'

The look that they exchanged in the ensuing moment, brief as it was, before Toni half-shrugged and turned away, was to come back to her many times. It was a fraught look, in which the half-formed realization of a wrong struggled against and drowned in a mutual helplessness, a complicity. In the moment of that look, she thought afterwards, something changed irrevocably between them, though what that something was, she could not say. Ned broke the silence with an abject, 'I'm sorry, Kid.'

But Toni could not believe that the little knife was gone. All that week, as the tongue keeps feeling for a missing tooth, she found herself drifting over to the antique letter-desk in the bedroom (one of their few indulgences, purchased with wedding-present money) and reaching into the cubbyhole where it had been kept. And when her hand did not find its cool, familiar shape, gracefully curved, pleasant to hold, her heart seemed to lurch and then to beat more heavily.

She never went near the ebony box. When they moved to a new apartment a couple of months later, it made its reappearance on Ned's bureau, a quiet appropriation she saw no reason to contest or comment on. And by the time they divorced, in another city, four years afterward, they had both come to think of the box as belonging to him. It was one of the few things he bothered to take.

3

The reclaiming of the knife did not, as Toni must somewhere

have feared, signal a withdrawal of Kayla's friendship. In fact, for a while, a new friendship blossomed among the four of them: Kayla and Dieter, reconciled, rented a tumbledown cottage in a part of town where rents were still cheap; Toni and Ned helped them plaster and paint, and soon rented an apartment not far away. There were dinner parties that spilled over into all-nighters and breakfasts in Chinatown, there were picnics and rooftop barbecues and marathon games of charades. They test-read scripts aloud to help Ned, now directing, select new original plays for the coming season; they listened to chapters of Dieter's still-unfinished novel, by this time running some four hundred pages. Toni rejoiced inwardly to see how intently Dieter listened to her comments, head on one side, eyes narrowed, smiling faintly; she had become one of them at last, it seemed, her contributions solicited, respected.

With Kayla, she played. They pasted a crazy collage of pictures cut from magazines all over the bathroom wall, they swung themselves sick on park swings, they went for long giddy walks in the rain. It was Kayla's way to knock on the door, any hour of the day or night, crying, 'Toni, do you remember play dough, from kindergarten? Remember how it smelled – good enough to eat? I found a recipe. Let's make some!' or, 'Toni, you've got to come outside, it's raining the most wonderful warm rain and the catkins are blowing down from the trees, they smell so beautiful, Toni, like tea! Come for a walk with me, you'll see, it's like being inside a giant teapot!'

Away from the house and from the men, they talked more, they exchanged confidences. Dieter still flew into rages, Kayla admitted, and he was threatening to quit working in her father's store – he thought *she* ought to be supporting *him*, at least until he finished his novel. Ned knew that the theatre company was on the verge of bankruptcy, Toni disclosed, but it was like he had blinkers on: he'd made no contingency plans and whenever she brought it up, he changed the subject. Kayla wondered whether *Horse of a Different Colour* had a prayer of getting published: she thought it was too long as it was, and Dieter claimed it was less than half finished. But then, countered Toni, Ned wasn't writing at all any more, he'd never finished a single play after his first one-act, he'd abandoned three attempts, each at an earlier stage than the previous one. At least Dieter hadn't lost his nerve.

Kayla thought it was only a matter of time before Ned started writing again – getting married had probably thrown him, men were like that. Toni assured Kayla that even if *Horse of a Different Colour* needed pruning, the good parts of it were engaging enough that some editor was bound to see its virtues sooner or later. Both relieved, they would hug each other and stroll on, scuffling through piles of autumn leaves; or they'd look at the bill, count their combined change, and order two more teas and a fries to share.

Charmed days, Toni thought later, and she recalled this period with a poignancy that made it seem in memory to have lasted much longer than it had – the way mist will magnify a tiny island. For that was what it turned out to be, a tiny island. That winter the theatre company did go broke, and Ned, jobless, still suffering from writer's block, sank progressively into a stupor in the corner armchair, where he thumbed through books on modern drama without reading them, or – worse – simply stared at a piece of the carpet until Toni thought she could see a worn spot in the nap where his eyes rested. He'd be in bed when she left in the morning, and in the armchair when she returned, sometimes still in his bathrobe. He barely greeted her.

Dieter and Kayla began to fight again, Dieter coming over to explain why he was throwing Kayla out, Kayla to explain why she was leaving him; then both, with a magnum of wine, to celebrate their decision to hang in after all; in a couple of weeks it would start all over again. Ned seemed to perk up when friends came by; this made it difficult for Toni to confess to anyone that she was worried about him, or to describe why. Kayla was the person she'd have been most inclined to tell, but she didn't want to burden Kayla when things seemed so rocky at their end. She kept hoping she was blowing it up out of proportion, that it was a passing mood, that soon something would turn up to get him moving again.

When her school term ended and Ned seemed no better, they packed up mostly at Toni's insistence and moved to a nearby city where there seemed to be an active enough theatre scene and where her thesis adviser had connections and had recommended her for a position it would have been silly to refuse. There, for a while, Ned rallied a little, made some contacts, did some freelance directing, and even began scribbling again. But it didn't last; again he seemed to lose heart, to grow remote, apathetic; she told him about job leads she'd heard of, he didn't follow up; she clipped announcements and jotted down the deadlines for playwriting competitions, he didn't submit anything. 'What do you *want*, exactly?' she asked him once, when in a rare communicative moment he'd hinted that the move had really not solved anything for him. For answer he only stared at her, apparently startled by the question. She realized he had not the faintest idea.

Kayla wrote that she'd split up with Dieter 'for real this time'. She'd been very ill, she wrote, but she was better now, she was living at her father's till she could afford her own place again, she had just started a new job at a florist's. She liked to work among plants, with the smell of earth and flowers around her – it was healing. Dieter had gone to Strasbourg to visit an uncle; he might come back to Canada in a few months, he might not. The letter was written in a large, childish scrawl, in smudged pencil, on the backs of two florist's invoices; these were folded together clumsily, page two on top, and stuffed into a crumpled, greyish envelope with the old address of her father's store, Sid's Shoe Palace, printed on it. Across the flap she had scribbled, 'I'll write you guys a real letter soon,' but nothing else came.

In town later that year to submit her thesis, Toni tried several evenings to reach Kayla at her father's, but there was never an answer. Finally she went by the shoe store in the daytime. Sid was there, she saw him through the window, shuffling papers by the cash, looking harassed. A bulky, frowning man who wore frayed sweaters, whose wide wavy fingernails were stained yellow with tobacco, whose uncombed greying hair stuck out in stiff tufts from his forehead and around his ears.

'Kayla? You want Kayla?' He peered closely at her, he did not recognize her, she'd met him only once or twice. He held up his hand for a second – 'Bring from the back, the black ones!' he called to an employee, a pimply-faced kid, who had just appeared from behind a curtain that hung in the stockroom doorway. 'Kayla, she's gone away for a visit, three-four weeks ago she left. What for do you want to see Kayla?'

'I'm only in town for a week. My husband and I used to live near her, we moved away around a year ago. She wrote to me that she was living at your house now.'

'Was for a while living by me.' He scowled. 'So, she wrote you. So, you know the story, that the husband went off.'

'Is that where Kayla went too – to Strasbourg?'

'What – she should chase him?' He rammed a staple through a pile of dirty invoices. 'Where she went, it's with a girlfriend, somewhere in the countryside she has a small house, so she invited Kayla she should come stay there as long as she likes. They don't have no telephone there, otherwise I would give you a number where to call.'

'What about an address?'

Looking at her sharply: 'You think she gives me?' And then he turned his face away, he shook his head. 'Kayla, Kayla.'

Toni cast through her mind to see if she could think of any woman they knew in common who had a country house: nobody she knew. But Kayla made friends easily and everywhere; this would be someone new. Over the next few days, she learned from friends that the illness Kayla had referred to was the result of a botched abortion. Kayla had nearly died; they'd had to do a hysterectomy. This much, everyone seemed to be agreed on, but the background was hazy. Some had it that Dieter had forced the abortion because he didn't want financial responsibility for a child; others said that Kayla had done it behind his back, and against his wishes, out of fear of her mother's illness. Whichever it was, Dieter had not been able to handle what followed, and had left for Europe while she was still in the hospital.

On the train going home, Toni wrote Kayla a letter saying she'd been in town, she'd heard something of what Kayla had been through, and she hoped that things were looking better now. What else did one say? She found herself unable to take in what she had been told, unable to get her head around it or her heart to comprehend it. She urged Kayla to come visit her and Ned any time. As she wrote this, she felt a pang of doubt; the pen hesitated; Ned had been increasingly reclusive and surly, she had no way of knowing what kind of host he might prove. Afternoon sun, flashing between the poles of the trackside power lines, flickered across the page she held balanced on a book on her knee. She was twenty-three, Kayla was twenty-seven; she felt their lives flying along separate tracks, no longer parallel. The railbed was uneven, her handwriting jerky. She would mail the letter to Kayla in care of her father, and hope it got to her eventually. She did that. There was no reply.

4

Either way, Toni thought, when she thought about it then or after, Dieter came out looking a cad. If he wanted to deny Kayla a child, or if he wanted to force her to have one that might be schizophrenic. But it was all hearsay, and the very fact that there were two versions made her wonder if there wasn't a third. She never found out, for the next time she saw Kayla – an accidental meeting three years later – it was not discussed. Kayla mentioned only the hysterectomy, and just in passing. 'I was glad,' she said in a stony voice, unlike the voice Toni remembered, 'People felt bad for me, but I'm glad it turned out the way it did. It put an end to that whole question for me, once and for all.'

They were sitting at a checker-clothed table in a restaurant adjacent the train station of a town about equidistant from the cities they lived in, a place not on the usual circuit for either of them. Kayla was returning from a rare visit to her mother, who had been placed in a new facility in the countryside. 'They don't call it an institution, they call it a facility,' she explained, 'because it facilitates things. Like, it makes it easier for you to explain to yourself why you don't visit much. The place is almost impossible to get to if you don't have a car.'

Toni, who had broken with Ned a year before, was here to change trains (service by direct route having been suspended due to a strike) en route to spend a long weekend with her lover. They'd met at an academic conference, eighteen months earlier; they were still stunned, still trying to explain it to each other, even while they made job applications and plotted ways to bring their lives into geographic conjunction. Toni was also, and on purpose, nearly four months pregnant, though she could not bring herself to tell this part of it to Kayla.

As it turned out she didn't get to tell Kayla much. She had only an hour till train time, and Kayla did most of the talking. 'I can't believe it's you,' Kayla cried as they embraced on the platform, breathless from having run towards each other in the shock of recognition. 'Toni, am I dreaming? Do you have any time? My train isn't till four. We could get lunch. I can't believe it, it's like you were sent to me. I've just been wandering around feeling like I wanted to die, and I look up and there you are.'

It was spring; vendors outside the station-house had set up stands of potted tulips and daffodils. Kayla ran over on impulse and bought one for Toni; the pink and yellow tulips sat on the table between them. 'Toni, how much money do you have? Can we order some wine? Look how one moment I'm wanting to die, and the next, there's something to celebrate – isn't that life? When I left the Home I was so upset that I hitched a ride going the wrong way, and didn't realize it for nearly ten minutes. The man was so nice, though, he turned around and drove me back. He drove me all the way here.'

The waitress took their orders for chicken salad sandwiches and a demi-litre of red wine. Kayla reached into her bag – a large cloth bag of the sort she always carried, it made Toni smile – and took out tobacco and rolling papers. As she spoke she rolled cigarettes with nimble, stained fingers, lining up the finished ones beside her napkin. 'I never talked to you about my mother in the old days, Toni, did I? After she went in the hospital to stay, when I was thirteen, my father used to take me with him to visit her, I don't know, maybe once or twice a month. Sometimes she would be happy to see us and we'd have a great time, laughing and singing – only, after, I'd fight with my father about why she couldn't come home. But other times she wouldn't talk to us, or she'd pretend not to know us – I don't know how I knew it was pretending, but I was sure it was. Sometimes she would just stare at the wall the whole time saying horrible things about us. We never knew how she was going to be. After a while I stopped going, I couldn't stand how upset it would make me if she was bad. I was mad at my father and I was mad at her – that was when I left home. I was sixteen or something.' She closed the tobacco, put it away, and lit one of the cigarettes. 'And then I saw her only once in a while, like maybe two or three times a year. And in the last few years, even less than that. Always with my father, though. I never went by myself, until a year or two ago.'

Their plates had arrived. Toni moved the tulips to make room; Kayla poured a glass of wine for herself and a glass for Toni. 'Wait, I can't drink all that. Here,' Toni poured most of hers back.

Kayla took several rapid sips and continued, 'The last three times I saw her, she didn't know me. Didn't know or pretended not to. Just sat like a stone, like I wasn't there. Do you know what that's like, Toni? When I was a kid I always thought if we just stayed long enough ... but my father would say: Leave her, let her be, it's no good. He would have to drag me away. But today – Toni, it was so amazing, I came into the lounge and nobody else was there, she was sitting in an arm-chair in the corner, and the sun was coming in the window right in that corner, lighting up her face. Her hair was a little wild, and she was wearing a bright orange robe with flowers, that I brought for her last time. She looked so beautiful, Toni. My mother is very beautiful. Like a gypsy. Her hair is still almost all jet black, she doesn't age. And she looked at me and smiled, such a wise gentle smile, not surprised, as though she'd been expecting me – and said in this calm, low voice, "Kayla Rose. My only daughter".'

Kayla sobbed suddenly. She put her face down on the table. But before Toni could react, she recovered herself, she raised her head and went on: 'I don't know how to describe this to you, but it felt like a miracle. Like we understood each other absolutely. We held hands, we both cried and laughed a bit, and then I started singing to her – a song she taught me when I was little, she joined in right away and sang it with me, she was so pleased that I remembered the words! And I gave her some fruit that I brought, some black cherries ... she always liked those, when she lived at home we used to eat them by the basket, her and me, sitting out on the balcony – seeing who could spit the stones the farthest. But then do you know what happened? *Do you know what happened?*'

Toni shook her head mutely. She felt as if she were dreaming: the strangeness of seeing Kayla again to begin with, a face from what had begun to feel like some remote past; the strangeness of circumstance, of her own life in transition; the haze of nervousness she always felt before seeing Phil again, as if she might arrive and find he wasn't who she thought he was at all, that it was all in her head, his loving her – that even now that she was carrying his child, the child he too wanted, they could wake up suddenly to find it all gone up in smoke. Her head felt swimmy. How to take in this story from Kayla, this story of Kayla's mother, someone who for Toni had existed before only third hand, a fact to file away, hardly a real person?

'And then this idiot nurse comes and starts yelling at me for going upstairs without checking in, like, don't I know the rules and blah blah blah. So I had to go downstairs again and sign in with the head nurse. And when I came back up – I was only gone a few minutes, Toni, but my mother's face was completely different. She told me that I was a witch and there were death spirits in me, and when I tried to hug her she screamed for the nurse to take me away. Just screamed and screamed. It was like – oh, a bad movie, Toni – two other nurses came and took me downstairs, like I couldn't walk by myself. They said I could try coming back later in the day, after she calmed down, but I just wanted to get out of there. What good do I do her, tell me. Toni, aren't you drinking any more of this wine? I'll finish it, then. I'm not hungry, here, eat my sandwich.'

She was flushed; Toni noticed as she pushed the plate across that her hand was shaking. 'Shouldn't you eat something?' she asked, but Kayla shook her head. 'I'd be sick. Tell me about yourself. Tell me about Ned. I can't believe you're not together any more.'

Toni hesitated. She and Ned weren't speaking, hadn't been for months. 'He's okay, I guess. He has some sort of job in an agency. He has a girlfriend. What about Dieter, do you ever hear from him?'

'He came back. We see each other sometimes, we even sleep together once in a while. We're still legally married, you know, we never got divorced. He's living in a fancy house with this older woman, a potter, really high-strung. He has a scar on his forehead where she broke a clay saucer over his head one time. He's proud of it.'

'Whatever happened with his book?'

'His runaway horse – can you believe he finished it? Eight hundred pages! Some friends of his who run a small press finally published it, but only about a hundred copies ever got distributed. The rest are sitting in boxes in their basement, not even bound. He rants about it, you know Dieter. But he's writing another one – better, I think. This dame has money – some fat settlement from her ex-husband.'

The windowpanes shivered as an approaching train came into sight. 'Oh, no, is that mine?' cried Toni. She glanced at her watch. 'No, but I'd better get moving. Kayla, can we write each other? Where are you living? Let me give you my address.'

Kayla scribbled it on her napkin. 'I can't give you mine, I

haven't got a place of my own right now.' She was staying with a friend, she explained, because she'd been evicted from her last place, but she wasn't going to be there much longer, it wasn't working. She didn't have a job either. 'I get by, you know, I do this and that. Sometimes I get welfare. You can write me care of my father.'

'I did that once,' Toni remembered. 'Did you ever get it?'

Kayla looked vague. 'When was that?' She folded the napkin and wrapped the remaining hand-rolled cigarettes in it. 'Oh, after Dieter went to Europe. I kind of didn't want to be in touch with anyone, then.' Suddenly she reached across the table, she took both of Toni's hands in hers and squeezed them. Her hands felt very cold. 'What a gift,' she said quietly. 'Seeing you again like this. Oh, Toni! Remember those walks in the rain? The crazy things we used to do?'

When she got off the train later that afternoon, Phil took her suitcase and the pot of tulips Toni had forgotten she was carrying. Always, when she saw him standing on the platform, unmistakably himself and real, scanning the train windows to catch a glimpse of her, she felt a rush of amazed gratitude that obliterated everything else.

'For me?' he asked, of the tulips – a little bemused, but pleased. Caught off guard, Toni looked at the flowers and managed to miss only a beat. It simplified things.

'For the weekend. For us,' she said.

5

She did write to Kayla, two or three times. She wrote when Noah was born, and again when she and Phil got legally married, which as it turned out was not until Noah was a year old and she was pregnant again, with Jordan. She sent a birth announcement when Jordan was born, with a scribble on the back noting their moving date and the postal address of the hundred-year-old farmhouse they'd just rented, a short commute from the college where Phil now taught. Later they were to buy this house, with help from Phil's parents.

No response ever came from Kayla, and in the fullness of those years – Jesse was to follow Jordan within twenty-eight months, and somehow (when she looks back she can hardly understand how) they were to convert an old cowbarn into a printshop and to found their own publishing co-operative – Toni had little chance to think about the past. Once in a while, extracting a particularly bulky manuscript from their post-office box in town, she thought of Dieter and half expected to see his name on the package – half hoped to, if only out of curiosity – but that never happened.

Of Ned, she heard occasionally from people who'd stayed in touch with them both. After their divorce he went through a succession of jobs, girlfriends, and therapies; it was rumoured that he had a gambling problem; later she heard (she found it hard to believe) that he was selling Amway. She congratulated herself for having had the good sense to get out early, for having seen the writing on the wall, for her presence of mind in seizing happiness for herself when it became plain Ned would never be a partner to her in courting it. That was how she explained it to herself – that it was Ned's choice in life not to be happy; and whatever it was that made a man that way was something she neither understood nor, at last, felt compelled to try to. Thus reduced, he became in her mind a stranger with whom she had once co-existed for five years in the illusion of marriage.

So when he phoned out of nowhere, one brilliant Sunday morning in June, ten years after their split-up, she was taken aback by the immediacy, the as-if-yesterday familiarity of his voice. Phil and the boys had gone off to see a neighbour's new colt; she was alone in the tidy kitchen, enjoying a second cup of coffee in the unaccustomed peace of the empty house before settling down to read proofs for their fall catalogue. A breeze blew in the screened door; sunlight wavered in dancing squares on the waxed pine planks of the floor. The ivy creeping across the leaded-glass windowpanes kept up a festive fluttering, like banners.

'Sorry to ring you up out of the blue like this, I don't mean to intrude on you,' came Ned's voice, as if from the next room (and she remembered suddenly, *He used to call me 'Kid'*). 'It's just that I wondered whether you'd heard about Dieter.'

'Dieter? No, what about him?'

'He's dead. He was killed last week.'

A freak accident, or maybe not an accident. He'd driven off a cliff in a rented car, alone, while on a reading tour in England. His second novel had just been published there. According to the news item, there was no evidence of intoxication.

It was you I thought of, right away, Toni wrote Kayla. *I don't know why hearing about it hit me so hard – maybe because I heard it from Ned and it was the first time I'd heard his voice in six or seven years. It brought so much back to me – like those evenings the four of us spent together, the summer you guys rented the house on Waverly. Painting those insanely high ceilings. And the doors, remember how many there were, how we thought we would never get done with them? And the dinners on the roof, the hilarious theatre games. I realize I've blocked out a lot of stuff from my early twenties, kind of buried it – the good along with the bad. How I would love to see you again, Kayla. Would you think of coming out to visit us here? We have more than enough room, and I know you would love this place.* She enclosed a snapshot of the three boys – they were nine, eight, and six – striking poses in the cherry tree. *Noah, Jesse, and Jordan, left to right,* she wrote on the back, and as an afterthought, seeing the red heads and freckled faces for a moment through Kayla's eyes, *They all take after their father, as I'm sure you'll figure out right away.* At first she was at a loss for where to send the letter; then she dug up her old address book. She could think of no reason why Sid would have moved.

Summer deepened its greens. For a few days she lived vividly the past, was steeped in it, pensive. Phil was attentive and kind, but when she tried to speak of it to him, she found she would quickly fall silent, overcome by the flood of recollection, preferring to be alone with it. Then, like an illness, like a spell in the weather, it passed. Her life reabsorbed her, reasserted its claims. By August the light had begun to change, the foliage was sparser. There was a hint of chill in the air, mornings and evenings. She began to haul out and weed through and reorganize the school clothes; Phil retired to his study after supper to work on fall course preparations. The boys' voices, up in the orchard or along the stream during their evening games, seemed to carry farther, to ring out with a heightened urgency.

When the letter arrived, she opened it unsuspecting. A squarish pink envelope of an odd size, like a leftover from an old set of boxed notecards. No return address; postmark from a city where she knew no one. It was addressed to her in black felt marker, untidy printed capitals slanting like a child's.

Inside, a single sheet of lined paper, torn raggedly off a small notepad. No heading, no date; a short message in green ballpoint, in handwriting that wasn't immediately familiar – for a split second she almost felt frightened, what could this be, a stranger's prank? a threat?

Dear Toni, she read, her heart pounding, *I'll be brief. I never liked you and I have no wish to see you again, now or at any time in the future. My own memories of the time you mentioned are not nice ones. That's all. Please don't write again. Kayla.*

* * *

She can recite the words from memory even now, years later; even though she destroyed the letter that same evening, crumpling it into the Franklin stove and watching the flames consume it from the edges. Even though you would think she'd have gotten it out of her system, that night and the several nights following, sobbing herself to sleep in Phil's arms. For a long time the memory of it, striking without warning, could still bring tears, turning her inward, making her remote, inaccessible, for a dark hour or two. But eventually she thought of it neutrally, dry-eyed; almost with wonder. It has taken its place as one of the enigmas of her life.

Janine

I LAY AWAKE late into the night with a twitch under my eyelid. It is hard to say whether the twitch was what was keeping me awake, or whether it was itself a symptom of my fatigue, for it had been several nights since I'd slept soundly. In any case the twitch wasn't helping.

My shifts and turnings, a vain attempt to find a position more conducive to sleep, disturbed my wife – a fact of which she apprised me by frequent shifts of her own, each accompanied by an exasperated sigh. Yet she did not seem at any point to come fully awake, which led me to wonder. I have trouble communicating with my wife even when I am awake, yet here she is able to deliver a clear message to me from the depths of slumber. It was the usual message: I wear her out, there is no peace with me around. I see that this is true.

After an hour or two of such sighs, it occurred to me that since I was not likely to fall asleep for a good while – if I managed it at all – I could at least ensure my wife a night's rest by removing myself to the guest bed in my study, where I could toss and turn to my heart's content, or, for that matter, switch on a lamp and read, if I so desired. But I had no sooner got myself settled there and shut the light, than my wife appeared in the doorway, ghostly in her flannel nightgown, her long hair in disarray, her face – such as I could make out in the light of a streetlamp shining in through the balcony door – distraught and puffy with sleep.

'Are you there, Robert?' she asked tensely. 'What are you doing sleeping in there? For heaven's sake – come back to bed.'

My eyelid, which had been quiet for a few minutes, began to jump again. I said, 'I have insomnia, I was only keeping you awake. You'll sleep better if I stay put.'

'What are you talking about, Robert? Don't be silly. What woke me was your leaving the bed. I woke up and you weren't there. It's jolting.'

Somehow I persuaded her to let me be. I told her I was going to read for a while, to make myself sleepy, and then I would come back to bed. She hesitated, it was clear that she didn't like it, but also that she was too sleepy, herself, to argue. I switched on the lamp and smiled at her benevolently. She went back to bed.

Then, so as not to make a liar of myself, I picked up a book from the top of a pile on the corner of my desk, where books that I mean to get around to reading are left to accumulate. This one was a recent release of a colleague of mine at the college – its flashy dust jacket proclaiming it 'a disturbing inside look at how our monolithic school system hobbles its teachers'. *Obstacle Courses* had garnered for him a surprising amount of attention from the press, and was still being talked about; I'd begun reading it before, but had to put it down because I was behind in my marking. Now my earlier, disagreeable impression was confirmed: the book had nothing to say that we hadn't all been saying for years, in acerbic undertones in the teachers' lounge; and it said it in a popular lingo that pandered to the media, trotting out every buzzword in currency. Moreover, it seized upon insights several of us had expressed over the years (I recognized my own, among others) without properly crediting any of us. Let's face it, any of a number of us could have written this book – I could have written it, and done a better job – but none of us thought to write it; and this not very exceptional man, this presumptuous *hack* with an eye for opportunity, was basking in epithets like 'boldly provocative' and 'on the cutting edge' simply because he had had the idea of committing to paper the everyday trade in wry observations, the apocryphal anecdotes, the lyric laments with which we teachers sweeten our between-class hours and spice our committee meetings. Which may be to say we others waste our eloquence, our critical intelligence, on air – where, but for our self-appointed spokesman, sitting back in the corner, listening and storing up, drawing out now you, now me, with his flattering probes – it would all be lost forever ...

But this thought was even more annoying to me than the book itself, occasioning from my eyelid a violent flutter like that of a trapped moth. I threw down the book, reached over once again to switch the lamp off, and in the moment of doing so, became suddenly and powerfully aware – I cannot tell you how – that there was somebody downstairs.

My skin crawled. I had always thought of this as a figure of speech, but at that moment I distinctly felt it lift and move, like an animal's pelt. The fact that there was nothing at all on which to base my inference – I had heard not a thing, nor was there any change in the atmosphere of the house, no light shining up the stairwell, no draught of air – seemed irrelevant: I knew that somebody was downstairs.

For a second or two I lay frozen. Then reason took over: I remembered locking up, and if someone had broken in, I would surely have heard something – having been awake all along. I had not heard anything; therefore, no one had broken in. It was a fact that I was overwrought from lack of sleep, and might as a result be prey to imaginings. It was, however, possible that someone with a key had come in quietly. Our daughter Lydie, who is twenty and moved out to an apartment of her own six months ago, still has a key. While I could not quite fathom why Lydie would come back to her parents' house in the middle of the night, it was not inconceivable. There were numerous possibilities: the heating or plumbing might have malfunctioned in her apartment (the place is a dump), she could have come home late from somewhere to find it had been broken into, or there could have been trouble with a neighbour. If Lydie had come home to us – being a good girl, a considerate girl – she would have made every effort not to awaken her mother or me. Knowing the house as one knows a place one has lived in most of one's life, she would have left her shoes in the vestibule, tiptoed in without turning on a light (the same streetlamp that illuminates my study shines in the front windows downstairs), skirted the creaky floorboard in the hall as she learned to do coming in late as a teenager, and curled up to sleep on the cushioned divan in the corner of the living-room.

As I ran this scenario through my head, it was as sharp and clear as though I watched it on a screen. I saw Lydie asleep on the divan, her long light hair fallen across her cheek, one arm dangling over the edge, curled fingers almost touching the carpet. Because she hadn't wanted to wake us, she was sleeping without a blanket. On went the lamp again. I pulled my bathrobe around me once more, scooped up the quilt that covered the guest bed, and tiptoed downstairs to tuck it around my daughter.

So convinced was I of the reality of what I had just imagined, that I stood a moment bewildered in front of the empty divan. Slowly it registered: Lydie wasn't here. Lydie hadn't come home. Why then was I standing in the living-room in the middle of the night with a twitch under my eyelid and a gingham quilt over my arm?

I dropped the quilt on the divan for the moment and went to check the front door. It was locked of course. I headed down the hall to check the back door, which is off the kitchen. And nearly jumped out of my skin.

The kitchen light was on. A woman was standing at the counter, making a peanut-butter sandwich. How do I describe the improbability of this moment? Every detail was absolutely compelling, as though to mock my incredulity. There was a crescent-shaped smear of jam on the white Formica countertop; for some reason, this is what I focused on, what I found myself staring at.

The woman was a woman that I knew. Knew? No, that wouldn't be fair to say. I didn't know her full name or her history or anything of the sort; but I knew her on sight, from the neighbourhood, I knew her face. She was a regular at the local restaurants, the various convenience stores; she was a fixture. Janine, I'd heard the proprietors call her; they all knew her. 'Time to go now, eh, Janine.' A big, dowdy blonde, maybe thirty-five, though she could have been younger, who'd touch you for a cigarette or spare change if you passed her on the street, and who'd walk right up to your table at the corner café and comment cheerfully on what you had on your plate. She did that once when I was having lunch there with my wife. Fernande spoke pleasantly to her and didn't seem fazed at all, but I was annoyed at the interruption, and annoyed at Fernande for prolonging it by encouraging the woman. Next thing, I thought, she'll be buying her lunch, asking her to sit down with us. Not that I would have begrudged her the lunch, you understand, but quite frankly, I haven't patience for small talk even with neighbours who have all their marbles.

With Janine, it was hard to say what it was exactly – she was childlike, but didn't look retarded, it was more that she lacked social inhibitions, talked ramblingly, projected a distressing aimlessness and chaos. She was unpredictable. Without thinking about it consciously, I suppose I had placed her in my mind as a psychiatric out-patient, one of the many that our hospital system can no longer accommodate – probably living on a welfare stipend that barely kept her, probably in a halfway house or apartment hotel (we have both in our neighbourhood, which has always been mixed), probably on medication. The hankering for a little society, no doubt, was what drove her out to linger for hours in the family-run stores and restaurants.

Now, inexplicably, Janine was in my kitchen in the middle of the night, fixing a peanut-butter sandwich. Moreover, when she noticed me, she seemed in no way startled or abashed. 'Ah! monsieur,' she exclaimed girlishly, waving the knife, 'maybe you are hungry, too. Would you like for me to make you a sandwich?'

Strangely, perhaps, my unmediated response was to feel pique at what I took for an attempt at subterfuge – as when one of my students, handing me a late term paper, tries to distract me by talking animatedly about something else. Only my reflexes as a teacher enabled me to get out any words at all. 'What I would like,' I said in a voice that surprised me by its evenness, 'is to know how you got into my house.'

It was Janine's turn to look surprised. 'But, monsieur!' she protested, reaching into her pocket and holding something up to show me, 'You don't remember? It was you, yourself, who gave me the key!'

For a moment my head swam. Was it possible, were there circumstances under which I could have given this woman – a stranger, and possibly crazy – a key to my house? No, the idea was patently absurd. The truth is that when Lydie moved out, when my own daughter moved out, I wanted her to give us back her house key. Yes. I didn't want her to feel she could come and go freely, once she had left the nest insisting that she wanted her independence. Let her have her independence, I thought, but let us have ours too. I wanted that symbolic gesture from her. But her mother defended her. Fernande said that I was being petty – 'petty and vindictive', those were her exact words – because Lydie wanted to move out. 'Lydie is my daughter,' she said, 'and my house will always be her house too, no matter where she happens to be living.' I felt ashamed then, and Lydie kept her key. Nor has she abused it; in fact, except to water the plants and check for mail when Fernande and I are away, I don't believe she has used it at all. Tonight, for instance, it turned out that she was not here, even though I would have been glad to see her. Janine was here instead.

Who, then, had given Janine a key, and the leave to make herself at home here? Would Fernande have done such a thing – and without telling me? Could my wife have befriended Janine, unbeknownst to me? How long had this been going on?

My head ached, my eyelid jumped, and suddenly all I wanted was to be back upstairs in my bedroom, snug in bed beside my wife, who is a better person than I am. I had the childish thought that if I switched off the kitchen light – just as though I had come in to check up and found nothing amiss – things would go back to normal and Janine would disappear, would turn out never to have been there. The light switch was within my reach. But I did not dare to flick it off; what if Janine were to cry out in surprise or alarm, waking my wife? Then the whole situation would have to be dealt with on the spot, and I did not feel equal to it. Let Janine have her midnight snack; I would go back to bed and hope that by morning she would be gone. If she was, then I could broach the subject cautiously with Fernande by light of day; if she wasn't, Fernande could deal with it. Fernande would know what to do.

I turned my back on the lighted kitchen and its occupant, and headed with quiet purpose for the stairs. I am convinced that under the circumstances, any sensible man would have done the same. After all, it had been several nights since I'd slept soundly, and a man deprived of sleep is in no condition to think clearly.

But where the stairs had been, there were now no stairs,

only a blank wall. I turned again, and noticed on the facing wall an unfamiliar door, the sight of which filled me at once with relief and hope. Opening it, I found myself gazing into the living room of my childhood home; a small scrubbed boy in pyjamas knelt on the carpet, playing with toys I recognized as mine.

He looked up, then, and I wanted to say something to him, but it was clear from his eyes that he didn't know me.

Deuxième Arabesque

SOMETIMES when you come in after dark, the woman is at the piano and is absorbed, and doesn't turn around, although you know she's heard you. You know by a change in the quality of the music, which when you came in was a little careless and slack, almost absent-minded, like a person who hasn't bothered to get dressed because it's the weekend – but suddenly takes on a vibrancy, the tension of a rope pulled taut, in the awareness of an audience. But when you come up quietly in your crepe-soled shoes to stand at her elbow, or when you stretch out full length on the couch nearby to listen – making a statement of your presence – a faltering begins: one false note, then another, till the piece like a tumbling card house falls apart, breaks down.

And then she turns to you; she says (in the disappointed quiet of the room) 'Hello, you're back.'

Her voice is low-pitched, shy, and resolute, abandoning the music to embrace you, relinquishing it for you. You know she's glad to see you; it shines in her eyes. You cannot measure what she has lost here – you do not try – but you feel the pieces of it still adrift in the room. You know that if you motion for her to go on, or to play again, she will shake her head; that's over, for tonight. Now she will serve the dinner she's kept warm for you, she will ask what kept you, she will give the rest of the evening over to you.

She is your own age, this woman; she is past forty. You have been married two years: the second time around, for both of you. But when she gets up from the piano stool and gives you her arm, reaching with the other hand to draw the curtain in the lamplit living-room, she seems a girl to you – as if the music had pulled her backward into girlhood and claimed a part of her that cannot ever entirely belong to you – and for some reason you are touched by this, and want not to disturb it; you are grateful that under your roof she feels safe enough to go back there.

Sometimes she laughs a low laugh and says 'You've spoiled it' when the music stumbles to a halt, but you feel no blame from her – only the faint regret of a child whose soap-bubble has broken on the wand. As a girl, and late into her teens, she played seriously, she has told you; they pulled her out of school, she was being groomed for a concert career. Something happened, then, and she abandoned it. She has never said what. You don't press her; you have an idea. You know that her teacher was a married man, then in his thirties – prominent, charismatic. She made a clean break – sold her piano, went away to live with an aunt and uncle in another city, finished school late. Then she went to work for the uncle, who owned a printing company. He found her capable and energetic, personable; he trained her in the business and was thinking of making her a partner when she shocked him by leaving to marry her first husband.

Of that disastrous first marriage, to a gifted but unstable young filmmaker whose early success was to be eroded by a series of mental breakdowns, Nonnie has said little. You know that the marriage was on the rocks by the time her daughter was born, and that it ended shortly after; you know that Ariane remembers nothing of her father, who committed suicide when she was two years old. They lived alone together, then, mother and daughter, all of Ariane's life before they came to you; and they came as a pair, so closely bonded that you still sometimes feel like an intruder in their world of unspoken sharing – of parallel, swiftly changing moods, delicate silences, enigmatic glances and gestures. Ariane is fifteen now, dark-haired and dark-eyed like her mother, similar in height and build – suddenly no longer a child. It troubles you that she sometimes borrows her mother's clothes, that you have once or twice recently come up behind her thinking she was Nonnie – about to embrace her, noticing your mistake just in time. It troubles you that with a dark look, the slam of a door, she can shatter her mother's composure for hours. This is new.

Nonnie at the piano: this, too, still new to you. Nonnie at the piano she bought years ago, not for herself but for Ariane, in the hope Ariane might play: and Ariane did play, for a few years, but without passion – working her way doggedly through the perennials that even you recognize, the Clementi sonatinas, Bach minuets and two-part inventions. Occasionally she will still sit down and pick through one of them, but only when her mother isn't around 'to get the wrong idea', as she says. Ariane has a guitar now, and she hunches on the edge of her bed and strums it in the evenings, her huge shadow jumping on the wall by flickering candlelight, her vocal accompaniment tentative, sweet-toned, a little off-key. You were the one who bought her the guitar: it was an offering, the beginning of a pact between you, this gift timed just right. And only when it became clear that Ariane had finished with the piano did Nonnie begin to edge back to it – here, under this roof, in your house. Furtively, at first – only when you were out – jumping away if you caught her at it. But now, increasingly, with an absorption that can tolerate an audience, that can survive interruption, an absorption you want to cheer on, to nurture, never to fracture ...

How do the fingers remember and recover what they learned so long ago? To you, who are not musical, it seems miraculous, though she tells you it is like swimming or riding a bicycle, one never really forgets. One by one she has begun to resurrect the pieces she used to play, chunks of them washing up whole, from memory, played over and over till she is driven to hunt up the score and fill in the gaps. Then sessions of frowning at the printed notes on frayed yellow pages crumbling at the edges, spines reinforced with brown brittle Scotch tape decades old. It is an archaeology that you are witness to here, a reconstruction.

Nonnie at the piano this summer evening, playing something you've never heard her play before: something cool and sprightly, luminous, like bouncing raindrops – the sound drifts out to you through the open window as you hoist the frame of your bicycle over your shoulder to carry it up the stairs. Ariane is away, you remember suddenly – gone to stay at a friend's cottage for a week; you and Nonnie will have these precious evenings alone together. With a bump you set the bicycle down in the front hall; you stand still in the arch of the living-room doorway, watching this woman you have chosen to live out the rest of your days with, this woman who has accepted to be your companion at mid-life. Her back is to you; she says, 'Hello, love,' in an abstracted voice, but continues to play – the music faltering for a second, then recovering itself and plunging on, phrases tumbling over each other like the tiers of a fountain, splashing and rippling. The light in the room, the last light of the day (one of the longest days of the year, you realize, just past the solstice) splashes and ripples too: late sunlight, orange-tinted, slanting through maple leaves at the window to make a shadow-dance on the wall above the piano, on the keyboard where Nonnie's hands are moving, across the back of her antique white blouse. Her dark hair is pulled back smoothly with a clip, but all around her head, picked out at this moment by the slanting sun, there stand out wisps and tendrils of shorter hairs that glint silver – turned hairs, growing in frizzly where she has abandoned the vanity of plucking them.

The music picks up energy suddenly, repeating an earlier figure, and presses to a startlingly abrupt ending – you are not sure at first if it's the end, but then Nonnie startles you, too, by whirling the piano stool – whirling all the way around once and then again on one spin, legs held up off the floor, balancing her upper body like a ballerina as she waits for the stool to come to rest.

Which it does, in a second or two, facing you.

'Did you hear that?' she asks, her face shining. 'It's a piece by Debussy I started learning when I was fifteen and never finished – never got past the first page of. It's two pieces, really – I learned the first one, but not the second. I've learned the whole thing now – just in the last couple of days – the first *new* thing I've learned. Do you like it?'

You tell her that you do. You tell her that you love to hear her play. You approach and stand above her – reach down, suddenly, and give the piano stool another twirl; she laughs and says, 'Don't, you'll make me dizzy,' but raises her legs again, obediently, and makes the circuit, tucking her head down so that when she comes to rest this time, facing away from you, the nape of her neck is there for your kiss.

Bending to it, you read on the music desk the title of the piece she has been playing: *Deuxième Arabesque.*

At My Left Hand Gabriel

THINGS WEREN'T RIGHT between them, it was clear to both. He had changed towards her, or she towards him; maybe they were both responsible. Or perhaps they'd been mistaken in each other to begin with. She was no longer devoted, he thought; she set his food before him absently, there was no care in it, her will was elsewhere. At one time there would have been flowers on the table, a clean cloth, small spoons standing ready in the cut-glass serving dishes of condiments she had spiced to his liking. Now she laid dinner not bothering with a cloth, on the bare table; and they ate with their heads lowered, in silence. He felt how her services to him had become a bondage, adhered to out of long habit, a form of empty duty. As to her, she felt sadly how she had ceased to believe in him somehow, had lost sight of what was fine in him, though she tried vainly, from season to season, to rekindle it in herself. She would look at him covertly in the evening when he sat in his chair under the reading lamp, one side of his face in shadow; she would scrutinize the familiar planes, the expanse of forehead where his hair had receded, the greying tufts at his temples, and he seemed to her like someone who has lost his power, someone irrevocably past his prime, though he was far from old. What was it she had once yearned toward, in that face – what had it promised her, that she felt he had not delivered, would not deliver? For she did feel there was a promise broken, somewhere, a trust not fulfilled. Once, she had believed in his greatness.

So they drifted along, more and more separate in that semblance or remembrance of marriage: he, remote, wrapped in his thoughts as though in a cloud, his innermost being hidden from her; she, caught up in the everyday, as is a woman's way, finding distraction in worldly life, absorbing herself in its coils. Yet they were always in each other's peripheral vision; that at least; one did not forget the other. And if the question lingered between them, *why go on like this, why not untie the tie and go our ways,* it lingered mutely, in their eyes only, it was never voiced between them. For he had chosen her, and she had loved him; and even in the cooling of their ardour, neither thought to look elsewhere.

But the unvoiced question deepened, from an occasional flicker to a low, persistent glow in whose light they now saw everything strangely coloured. And in the fall of that year, she began suddenly to speak of Gabriel.

'Why don't we hear from him, do you suppose?' she would ask, turning towards him briefly in the midst of some task she had occupied herself with. 'It's been so long – years – do you realize? I can't even remember the last time he visited. Oh, if only he would come now! If only he would just knock on the door and be standing there in the hall with his rucksack and his sleeping-bag, the way he used to! Mel. Do you remember?'

He remembered. It was true that their times with Gabriel, however ephemeral, stood out in memory as numinous somehow, filled with a grace that lingered afterward like a scent or a song, even days after he'd left them. For their friend Gabriel – friend of their earliest days – came and went according to his own designs: a wanderer, the only thing you could count on with him was that he wouldn't be staying long. 'Fish and company,' he would remind them gravely, though his eyes danced, 'both spoil after three days,' and so saying, he would roll up his pallet, pull on his weather-faded lumberjack shirt, and extend a hand to each of them in turn, in farewell. And then it would be months, or longer, before they saw him again – though now and then a postcard would arrive, or a gnomic letter scrawled on a paper napkin in a roadside diner, or a quite unexpected and lovely gift – a handful of tiny seashells from the Gulf of Mexico – a bowl hand-carved from drift-wood – a polished agate. What propelled him from one place to another, where he found his bread, how he spent his days – these were questions they never asked him; they had met him on the road, at a time when the road was a way of life for many of their generation; where others had come to rest at some point, and established lives for themselves, Gabriel went on in the old ways, a meditater and a drifter – a casualty, accord-ing to one view – a kind of saint, according to another. Amy was of the second school.

He did think Amy romanticized the man somewhat; always had. The gifts, when they arrived, meant something more to her; he had seen her run her hand over the contours of the wooden bowl, or hold the agate in her palm and gaze as though at a crystal ball, and had felt a twinge of irritation at her absorption – dreamy, reverential, as though through these objects she experienced a communion with the giver – as though she received some nourishment thereby. She loved Gabriel in a way, it was clear, but he had never felt jealousy over this love; there was something naive about it, so that it seemed innocent to him, and besides, in Gabriel's demeanour towards her there was nothing that offended him or tripped his alarms. Towards Amy, Gabriel was courtly – affectionate, no question, yet with a curiously distanced, ethereal quality to his affection, an absence of sexual import, that dignified what might otherwise have been called a flirtation, and made it somehow becoming, even poetic.

– But just now, she did go on. And it *had* been years. Why should she speak with such intensity of Gabriel now, when Gabriel had, as it were, absented himself from the picture for so long – when they had all but ceased to think of him as a presence in their lives, an individual still in their frame of reference? Hadn't he become a kind of shadow figure, almost more imagined than real – didn't Amy dream him, as much as remember him? And what was she on about, suddenly, with this insistence on missing Gabriel, this hankering for him to put in an appearance? Almost as though that were all that lacked for their life together to make sense again, for things to go back to some way that they had been before, or forward into some new harmony. There was a feverishness to her longing that almost infected him too, yet he held aloof from it; it seemed childish to him, simplistic; it was magical thinking. Yet in Amy's face at these moments, he caught something of the lovely animation, the fervent spirit, that had drawn him towards her in the beginning; and almost, he hoped.

And then, as if on cue, a letter came. 'You see!' she cried, triumphant – as though he'd argued (he never had) that Gabriel had forgotten them; as though she'd claimed (she never had) that by sheer will she could bring him back. She did seem to credit herself with this. A letter came: brief, in the way of all of Gabriel's communications, addressing them as 'Dear friends' – invoking the memory of old times shared – informing them, to her visible joy, that he was not far away. 'I have found a country retreat,' he wrote, 'a cabin halfway up a mountain, whose owner no longer uses it, and who is happy to have me occupy it and do some upkeep, for as long as I want to stay. So I have moved in and patched up the walls some, and laid in a supply of wood for winter. I find the quiet speaks to me here, it is very deep, I have no need to venture far beyond my small clearing. I am, I guess, not more than a three hours' drive from you, then a hike of maybe twenty minutes up the hill, along a clear trail. The view from here is something else.' And he had drawn a little map. He did not invite them to visit, because it was not Gabriel's way to ask things of others; but he had drawn this little map, which told them they were welcome if they wanted to make the journey, and told them it was unlikely that he would come to them.

'If the mountain will not come to Mahomet,' Mel said, wryly. He saw that there would be no peace with Amy until they went. He saw that she took this, Gabriel's reappearance, for a portent, and his tacit invitation for a test, and that there would be no peace unless they heeded what was, to her, an unmistakable signal.

'Why *should* he come to us,' she rejoined, already defensive, 'he's always come to us, because he's always been on the move, and we couldn't have known where to find him; but this time he's told us where he is and even how to get there.'

'*And* that the view from there is something else.' He was sorry as soon as he said it, he had not entirely intended the sarcasm he heard in his own voice; and Amy averted her face, as much, it seemed, embarrassed for him as injured herself.

'When would you like to go?' he asked, more gently; and at this, looking him full in the face, she replied steadily, 'Now.'

They set out that weekend, with Gabriel's hand-drawn map on the dashboard. It was a brilliant October day, but it had rained during the night and when they left, the pavement was still wet; freshly fallen yellow leaves were plastered on it, singly and in mats. Leaves clung to the windshield and had caught on the wipers; Mel reached around and peeled them off while the engine warmed. As they pulled out, early sunlight bounced off a crescent-shaped nick in the glass where a rock had struck it last summer; it made a sudden spangle, a prism that danced in Amy's eyes.

The road steamed softly ahead of them as the sun climbed. By the time they reached the highway, the asphalt was dry, but the turned fields on either side steamed faintly, dark clods of wet loam lying in moulded lumps, the puddled furrows reflecting bright flashes of sky. Everywhere the trees were fully turned and had begun to release their leaves; as the city receded, foliage grew sparser, and here and there a tree stood completely bare, or held out like a beacon a lone cluster of flaming branches mysteriously untouched by the winds that had stripped the rest. Half drowsing, the sun warm on one side of her face, Amy thought: there are parts of me inside that are like those branches, absolutely alive and burning, and I must hold on to them somehow. The thought came idly, but even in her sleepiness it struck her as substantial, something to return to later, if she remembered ... but already it was slipping away from her, entangling itself with floating ribbons of thought and nonsense that chased through her head, transient as the rainbow on the windshield which she seemed now to see again, winking between her eyelashes, as she nodded off.

She dreamed that she was walking with Gabriel beside a stream, along marshy ground that sank beneath her feet. Suddenly she felt water seeping in through the seams of her shoes. She looked ahead for drier ground and seeing none, hesitated; but Gabriel, seeming to read her mind, pointed to his own feet, which were bare. 'If you take your shoes off,' he told her in a wonderfully gentle voice, 'your feet will still be wet, but you won't mind it.' She laughed out loud at the solution, it was so simple; but once her shoes were off, she realized she had no knapsack to put them in, and Gabriel, also, was without a knapsack. 'How shall I carry them?' she wondered aloud, but he shook his head at her, smiling, and said, 'Why would you want to carry them? Leave them here; we'll come back the same way.' Amy saw a tree-stump just off the path, and went to put her shoes on it, but when she got there she saw that it was not a tree-stump at all; it was Mel's round hassock of shabby brown leather, that he used as a footstool for his reading chair. What a place for him to have left it, she thought; now we'll have to carry it back with us, and it's so heavy. For the hassock was an old one that had been a long time in the family; it was a nuisance to vacuum around, because it weighed so much, and it always left a round mark sunk into the carpet where it had sat. She turned to tell Gabriel, but he wasn't where she had left him on the path; he had walked on and was now far ahead, the red of his lumberjack shirt flashing between the dark trunks of trees.

Then she was awake, sun flashing in her eyes as they sped past dense pine woods. She had unlaced and slipped out of her hiking boots on getting into the car; a cool draft from the air vent was blowing on her stockinged feet, chilling them. She slid them back into the boots and redirected the air stream, away from her legs. 'Where are we?' she asked Mel.

For a moment he didn't reply; he was lost in his own thoughts. Then: 'We crossed the state border a few minutes ago.' And again he was silent. He didn't talk to her very much, this husband of hers at the wheel, taking her where she had asked to go. He didn't talk to her though he was a man of words, a man who had found his livelihood in words and who seemed to pour his very being into them; at one time he had talked to her often and at length, but this had changed. She glanced sideways at him now and wondered: When was it that he stopped talking to me? Did I stop hearing him because he wasn't saying anything new – is it possible he stopped talking because he saw I wasn't listening? And it seemed to her that both were true. He had ceased to say anything new, and she had allowed her mind to wander. And the result was that now he said nothing at all. Why should he speak to someone whose mind was elsewhere? But it's he whose mind is elsewhere! she protested to herself, surprised by her own train of thought; it's he who has wrapped himself in a cloud of remoteness, acting as though his thoughts were too lofty to share with me. And a sadness came over her suddenly.

So they rode in silence, until before long the road signs began announcing their exit, and they sat up straighter, watching for it. Not far off the highway they stopped to study Gabriel's map for landmarks, and drove on in anticipation of them: first, a roadside stand (where they pulled over and bought, as offerings, unfermented cider and a stoneware jar of apple butter) – then a ruined barn and a boarded-up farm-house; then a covered bridge. A little beyond was their next turn-off, this time onto a dirt road that began at once, with many twists and turns, to climb a densely wooded hillside. Cooler air, smelling of damp bark and earth, of pine and wet oak leaves, seeped into the car. Amy rolled her window down and breathed deeply. The sun was suddenly gone. Against a sky turned smoky grey, the yellows and russets of deciduous trees took on a sombre glow; the pines looked almost black.

How quickly everything has changed, she thought, and aloud she said, 'When did the sun go away? It's as if this road has its own weather.'

'Some places do,' Mel said briefly. Then, unexpectedly, he stopped the car and threw it into reverse, backtracking slowly along the wide curve they'd just taken. 'That must have been it – the place he marked on the map for us to park the car.' It was a flat, bulldozed area, large enough for two or three vehicles, sparsely gravelled and grown over with weeds now yellowed and lying on the ground. On a rotting post a derelict mailbox hung askew. They pulled in. With the engine shut off, the silence was engulfing.

'Are you sure this is it? Where's his car?'

'He might not have one.'

They sat, contemplating that. Gabriel had been once around the world by the grace of his thumb; probably he didn't have one. They sat listening to the engine ticking as it cooled. Stiffness from sitting had made them reluctant. 'Well,' Mel said finally. 'Ready to walk?'

'If you really think this is the place.' They got out, unkink-ing their legs, and she helped him fit the cider jug and the crock of apple butter into his knapsack, then slung her own smaller bag over her shoulder. He was studying the map again. 'We'll know soon enough: we should come to a big rock,' he said, and showed her where Gabriel had drawn an X, about a third of the way up the trail, printing beside it in a minute hand, 'Table rock – good lookout'.

But Amy had seen something else. 'I know now,' she announced. Half-hidden in the bracken at the start of the trail was a bicycle, the frame and build of a vintage that looked ancient, though newly painted a bright red. 'Look – those must be his wheels. Who but Gabriel?' And Mel, after a startled second, laughed: 'You're right.'

The trail was a steep upgrade, along shelves of pinkish granite and black mica half buried in moss and layers of old pine needles. The air was damp, fragrant with a sweet decay that brooded new growth. Here and there a pheasant rose whirring and churning the fallen leaves, flushed from its cover by their passage. Within minutes Amy was breathless, and paused to rest. 'I'm out of shape,' she laughed ruefully.

Mel slowed for her. He was kind, she reflected, even in his distance; he was kind to bring her here, and to pace himself to her, so that in semblance, at least, they walked together. But, did he not ferry her and wait for her the way a father, steeped in his private cares, attends his child – seeing her movements from the corner of his eye, responding automatically, almost without involvement? He was there with her, but was *he* there with her? She thought that in his presence, what she felt was his absence, and that made her sad. Yet she knew him to be kind.

Gabriel's lookout loomed ahead, a massive flat-topped boulder to the left of the path. From the front it presented as a wall, but around one side, they found a series of step-like ledges. They set their packs on the ground, climbed to the top, and turned to look back.

That was when they saw that the damp they breathed was a mist that had crept up behind them from the bottom of the valley, obscuring much of the vista and blowing in patches across what remained. Clouds covered the top of the range of hills that faced them; in the nearer distance, between bands of white opacity, they had a glimpse of water and of autumn foliage – but a glimpse that teased more than it informed. From here on as they climbed the trail, they felt the mist at their backs – they felt it encroach and overtake them, so when at last they came upon the cabin in its clearing, they saw it dimly, through a veil of milky white that magnified the dark shapes of the pines around it, the woodpile under a slanted roof of corrugated tin, the chopping-block with lodged axe pointing haft upward. All was still. A fine rain had begun to fall. No one came out to greet them.

No one answered to their knock. They tramped around to the back of the cabin, past the small privy whose door hung open, showing it empty. They called; their voices came back to them from across the misty distance. Could it be that after all this, Gabriel was not here? The possibility had never entered Amy's mind; she looked at her husband in dismay. For answer he shrugged, and motioned with his head toward the cabin: 'We'll go in and wait. How far away can he be?' The rain was coming down harder now, and they crossed the porch and ducked inside gratefully.

The cabin's interior, one large room, was roughly finished. At the center a primitive staircase, really not much more than a ladder, ascended to a sleeping loft. A wood heating stove clearly doubled as cookstove; pots and utensils hung near it from a low beam, and a large enamel kettle sat on top. Did their eyes trick them in the dimness, or was it steaming a little? There was a round table with three mismatched chairs, two of them missing their backs. There was an ancient, lumpy-looking sofa of brocaded material, with the legs removed; small barrels flanked it as end tables. On them were oil lamps and the remains of candles. The uneven floor was layered with pieces of old carpeting in different patterns, all of them faded. Rough-built shelving along one wall held jars of rice, dried beans, and various grains; along another, clothing hung on hooks. There was a kind of scullery – an alcove with a sink-basin built in, and a long-handled pump for water. There was a smell: an old countryhouse smell of damp, of leafmould and faint mildew, and the reek of kerosene, overlaid with woodsmoke that had permeated everything; traces, also, of a tangy fragrance, perhaps one of the herbs that hung drying in bunches from the ceiling-beams.

It was a Spartan space, yet not comfortless: tranquillity breathed from it, and a reassuring sense of order. 'We must just have missed him,' Mel said, stooping by the stove. 'The fire is barely out. The coals are still warm.' The water in the kettle was hot enough for tea, as though even in his absence Gabriel welcomed them. Mel found matches in a ceramic pot and rekindled a fire; Amy found a chipped brown teapot and two mugs, and pulled down a handful of dried mint leaves from one of the hanging bunches. They sat at the round table and sipped from the steaming mugs. The fragrance of the mint tea, which in recent years they seldom drank, was strangely evocative, soothing to her.

Gabriel could not be far. Perhaps he'd gone fishing; it was trout season – in the old days Gabriel had loved to fish, though he wrestled with the idea of it, he was otherwise vegetarian. And this was trout country. Yes, no doubt he was fishing some secret pool he knew of, some hollow scooped out of the bedrock of a small stream twisting down the hillside. Any moment now they would hear his footstep on the wooden porch boards, they would feel the floor tremble faintly announcing his return. He would come in, rain-soaked, shaking back his wet hair. He would come in with a catch of fish or without one; leaving his boots by the door, would peel off his heavy shirt and hang it on a nail above the stove; soon it would give off a warm, damp odour of wool saturated in sweet woodsmoke and clean sweat. He would show no surprise at seeing them, but a shy, calm pleasure would dawn in his eyes; he would say quietly, as though it were all that needed to be said after all this time, 'Well.' And then with quickening warmth – maybe with his easy, familiar laugh, '*Well.*'

This is as far as Amy wants to think it as they sit there, listening to the rain beat on the cabin roof, listening to it chime like steel drums on the tin overhang of the porch and the scullery window. The larger window in front of them faces the valley, but mist has by now drawn a thick curtain across the entire vista, and they look out upon white emptiness. It's as far as she wants to think it as they sit on in silence through the slow waning of the afternoon, while the anticipated footfall does not come – their friend does not come. Surely, though, he will return by nightfall, and all will be well – all will be, then, as she has hoped. The quiet in this place is healing, woven of gentle musics – the sighing of the pines outside the window as they heave in the rainy wind, the static of sparks ticking in the chimney-pipe, the diminishing horse-hooves of the rain. And it is as though Gabriel becomes their meditation as they wait beneath his roof, each in their separate space.

It may be that if she were to turn to him now, if she were to summon it of herself to speak bravely to Mel in a real voice, her own voice, in the voice of the woman she has become – that he would answer her, and a new conversation between them could begin. It may be. But she will not do this, because she is waiting for Gabriel. She is waiting for Gabriel in whose coming all differences – all distances – will dissolve.

And Mel, what is he thinking as the hours pass? Does he feel that time is wasting, that she has wasted his time in bringing him here to wait with her? or does he find his own solace in the waiting? Towards dusk he grows restless, the rain has let up, he goes outside to walk around. The grasses are tousled and sweet-smelling, bent with rain. She thinks that he will come back with Gabriel, but he comes back by himself; she has already lit the oil lamps, darkness is falling, he says nothing. Clumsy in the unfamiliar space, slow to find what she needs, Amy prepares supper, a simple rice dish, sweetened with a little of the cider they brought; she prepares enough for three, but only the two of them sit down to table. Gabriel has stopped the night somewhere, then, at some country neighbour's; surely at first light he will head homeward, when he can see his way, when he can more easily catch a ride. They'll wait the night.

They wash up and sit for a while longer, until the flickering of the kerosene light makes them drowsy; then they ascend with a lamp to the sleeping loft, find bedding in a chest by the top of the stairs, and make up places for themselves. Mel blows out the lamp and they sleep, waking briefly and separately in the night to the sound of renewed rain on the roof, or to the rustling of mice in the walls, or animal cries in the darkness beyond the cabin. In the grey of dawn Amy opens her eyes and sees Gabriel's bed still empty, made up as neatly as a soldier's bed, the heavy camp blanket tucked tight at the corners.

It is not really as though she expected him to arrive in the middle of the night. No, she cannot have expected that.

Their bones ache from sleeping on thin mattresses on the plank floor; their muscles ache from the chill in the cabin. They descend to the room below and Mel starts up the fire. No change in the weather: rain ticking against the glass, the window giving on the same white blankness, even the pine trees near the house are reduced to shadows in the fog. Again Amy boils water in the rice pot, and cooks oatmeal – enough for three – still hopeful, pleased because she has found powdered milk to mix up and serve with it, and she has found honey to sweeten it, and raisins. But again they eat by themselves, having waited until the cereal was beginning to congeal into a glutinous mass in its pot at the back of the stove. The morning wears on and the fog does not lift and Gabriel does not come.

Outside, though the rain has abated, everything is sodden, dripping; yellow leaves are pasted to the porch boards darkened with water. The walk to the privy and back soaks one's clothing. Now and again a bluejay touches down on a pine bough, then leaves it, screaming – the strident call piercing the mist, echoing faintly.

It may be that Gabriel is on his way home now, that he is at every moment drawing nearer. A dozen times Amy thinks she hears him on the porch, then there is no one. And, she has to admit, it may equally be that he has gone off somewhere for a few days – no way of knowing where or for how long, or even roughly when to expect him back. She doesn't like to think this, but it's in the air.

Finally: 'How much longer does it make sense to wait?' asks Mel. And in response to what he sees in her eyes as she struggles to answer: 'Amy. We could be here for days.'

'No, I know,' she says in a diminished voice, like a rain-drenched bird, 'it's up to you,' – but he thinks that he can still hear a pleading.

'Amy.' He tries again, he controls his own voice. 'Do you think that I can make him come?'

He is right of course. 'No,' she agrees at last.

A little later they take up their packs and descend the trail to the car, moving slowly into the obscuring cloud that hangs before them like a wall. Not once has it lifted to disclose the view Gabriel praised so highly. Yet she cannot shake the sense that he walks beside them now, a good host, drawing out the visit by seeing them safely to the road. The forest drips softly all around them, and a sweetness breathes from the dying ground.

Looking For My Keys

IT WAS ON FRIDAY AFTERNOON that I lost my keys, somewhere between home and the regular round of streets where I
do my errands. That is to say, I had my keys with me when I
left my house, on foot, to do my errands, and I did not have
them when I returned.

It is important, I think, to understand that we are not talking here about a person who loses keys. I do not lose keys. My
children lose keys, I yell at them about it, recently they've gotten a little better – I think I only had to make two replace-
ments this year. As to myself, I lose hats sometimes, I lose
gloves; umbrellas I lose almost religiously, and I have even
been known to lose single shoes, if such a thing can be imagined; but I do not lose keys. If by chance I misplace them,
they are quick to turn up; if I happen to leave them somewhere – very unusual – I remember where, almost as soon as I
miss them; and when I go back for them – there they are.

The closest I ever came to losing my keys before this was
one day about five years ago, coming home from Berman
Paint where I'd gone to buy a half-gallon of peach-coloured
furniture enamel to paint my kitchen table. I had meant to
paint the kitchen table, which was a horrible tomato-soup
colour, for years – not only because it needed a paint job (having been bought second-hand and a little banged up), but
because it clashed with the masonite countertop in the
kitchen of my rented flat. The countertop was a pebbled
shade of more or less salmon pink, a difficult shade to match,
and I had often had the thought that if I could only find paint
that colour, both the table and the counter would be happier
and the kitchen would take on a positively rosy glow.

But I could not very well take the kitchen counter with me to Mrs Berman's store, and painting the table was not enough of a priority for me to remember, in passing the paint store (which I did frequently), to go in and ask for a book of colour samples to bring home. So years went by. In fact, I had almost stopped noticing that the table clashed with the counter and that it needed painting, when someone gave me a gift: a peach-coloured coffee mug. This, when placed on the counter, appeared to exactly match it.

I was depressed at the time, let's not go into why, and when I am depressed, I like to do a little something to fix up my immediate surroundings – say, get rid of a constant low-grade irritant like a leaky faucet or a sticking door, put up a shelf where a shelf has long been needed, wash windows, buy a cheap lamp for a dingy corner. So, now that I had something portable that matched the elusive pink of the countertop, it seemed like a good time to paint the kitchen table. I saw at once that I could take the coffee mug to Mrs Berman's.

Let me explain that the particular habit I have developed of carrying my keys accounts both for the fact that I so seldom lose them, and also for how I happened to lose them this time. I carry my keys in my purse if I am away from the house for an extended period; but if I am just out briefly, on a neighbourhood errand, I don't like to have to bother, on my return, to fish around in my purse (which is large and full of all kinds of things) on the front stoop. So I carry my keys in my hand. No, I carry them *on* my hand. I slip the keyring, which is a perfectly plain ring, no doodads, over my index finger, where it fits comfortably and not too loosely; and I grasp the keys lightly in my palm. I find the feel of them comforting, like worry-beads. Also, I read somewhere in a magazine that if a woman walking alone at night carries her keyring in her palm, keys slipped between her fingers can make a spiked fist with which to surprise and fend off an attacker, if need be.

Actually, I have tried this — making the spiked fist, I mean; fortunately the occasion has not arisen for me to test it — and I find it a little awkward. Besides, could I ever bring myself to ram this fistful of metal into human flesh? But, in theory, it is one more reason to carry my keys the way I do.

If it happens that I need my hands, I slip the keys into my purse. Thus, if my keys are not on my finger, where I can easily see and feel them, then I know that they must be in my purse; I make it a point never to put them down anywhere else, if I am not at home. That way it is not easy for me to lose my keys.

Once not long ago, on the way home from the pharmacy, I realized that my keys were not in my hand, and as I turned up my block, I began feeling around for them in my purse and did not find them. I turned around straight away and retraced my steps: the pharmacy; before that, the post office; before that, the bank. My keys were not in any of those places. I was surprised and alarmed. It occurred to me that while I was in the post office, I had had to submit a claim card for a parcel, and then I had had to sign for the parcel; and that both the card and the parcel had my address on them, and that behind me there had been a line-up of people. There is usually a line-up of people in the post office, especially since they closed the branch at the photocopy centre and everybody has to go to the one in the stationery store.

Perhaps I had put down my keys on the counter while I signed for the parcel. It was unlikely, but I am sometimes absent-minded. Then someone standing behind me could have quietly pocketed my keys, having made a mental note of my address by glancing at the parcel. People are desperate these days; you see them everywhere, going through waste bins for bottles to return for cash, scavenging for useable items. My friend told me that sometimes at night, when he goes to drop off paper or bottles at the recycling bins, he will see a person fishing papers out of the paper bin (that's when the bin is full enough for a person's hand to reach paper, but it usually is, because they are so slow to empty the bins in this backward metropolis) – he will see a person systematically sifting through papers and checking out the addresses on certain envelopes. It's easy to recognize a government envelope, and in this way a person can tell who receives government cheques by mail, and where in the neighbourhood they live, and what day of the month the cheques get mailed on. Even if I had such information, I would not know to what practical use it could be put, but some persons can apparently use such information. And obviously a person who knew my address could make use of my keys, whereas one who did not, could not.

It happened, though, that on that particular occasion, I returned home to find that I had not had my keys with me to begin with: they were sitting on my desk, in plain view. And then I remembered that I had left the house in a hurry, in company of my friend, and that he had locked the door behind us with *his* key, and I had not bothered to check to make sure I had mine with me; I had simply assumed my keys were in my purse.

I was greatly relieved. I don't like to feel mistrustful of people, ordinary people who live in my quarter and stand behind me in the post office line. It hurts me to feel I can't trust people. During the years when I lived alone – I say 'alone' but I always had my children with me of course – I was not careful about the door, I didn't have the habit of locking it when I was at home, even after dark – at least not until I was ready to go to sleep, which in those days was often not until very late. It was my friend who, in the months when we began seeing each other, used to telephone me in the evenings to ask me sternly whether my front door was locked – this, once he had come to know my habits. At first it irritated me; I used to tell him shortly that I had lived in this neighbourhood all of my adult life and had never kept my door locked when I was at home and awake, and that it was for me to decide when to lock my door in the evenings. This was not, I argued, an American city; not like the cities he was used to. But I knew that he had a point, that the city was changing. And something in his protectiveness won me over. I began locking my door obediently when he told me to, and then I began locking it routinely on arriving home; and I felt, not that the locked door protected me, but that in obeying the voice of my friend in my head, telling me to lock it, I was entering a safe harbour of a kind, and accepting a great blessing that had descended, unasked-for, upon my life.

Now that I live with my friend, I can be more casual. I feel safe with him, and anyway, if I forget to lock the door, I can be pretty sure that he will do it.

The day I went to Berman Paint, you may have figured this out for yourself, what threw me was the coffee mug. Not on the way there, though. On the way there, I carried the mug in my purse – it just fit, and the purse still closed. I smiled to myself when I thought of opening my bag, taking out the coffee mug, putting it down on the counter in front of Mrs Berman, and asking for furniture paint to match it. Would she imagine that I was painting my table to match my coffee cup? Would she find that eccentric? Mrs Berman didn't turn a hair, she only smiled very faintly. She is an older lady and since Mr Berman passed away several years ago, she runs the store by herself. She is a person of few words, and nothing ever seems to surprise her.

I thought of explaining that I had brought the cup because it matched the counter and that I really wanted to paint the table to match the counter, but it seemed too complicated. People don't want to know the 'why' of what you do; it tires them. Mrs Berman reached behind her and took a sample book down from the shelf and opened it to a page of rose, orange, and pink squares. She moved the coffee mug slowly down the page and stopped at Dewy Peach, then moved it across the page to Coral Dust, then back again.

'Which do you think?'

'It looks a little light,' I said of Dewy Peach.

'They always dry darker.'

'They're both pretty close,' I said. If I had had the sample book at home, I could have decided, but since I was in the store, I looked to Mrs Berman to be the expert.

Mrs Berman pursed her lips briefly and said, 'The other one might dry too dark.' She went in back, to mix my colour. Then, since I was paying by credit card anyway, in addition to my paint I decided to buy a few other things: sandpaper, a gallon can of solvent, a couple of new brushes, a can of Varathane I had various uses for, some sealer for around the kitchen sink. Mrs Berman put it all in two plastic shopping bags. 'Can you manage?'

I carried a bag in each hand and my purse slung over my shoulder. 'Don't forget your cup,' said Mrs Berman. Since my purse was already zipped up, I slipped the handle of my coffee mug over my finger.

The door to my house wasn't locked when I returned, because my children were out on the front steps, talking to their friends. So it wasn't until later in the day that I missed my keys. I cast through my mind, the only place I'd been all day was Mrs Berman's, so I telephoned the paint store, confident that I must have left my keys on the counter while signing the credit card slip. But Mrs Berman said no, she hadn't found any keys. She put me on hold while she checked again – the counter, the floor around the counter. No, she told me again, no keys.

Then I did what I always tell my children to do when they

misplace a thing: I went over in my mind every detail I could remember of my trip to the paint store and back. And I realized almost at once that the coffee mug – the fact that I had left the store with it hung over my finger – would be a clue. Wouldn't I have been carrying my keys over the same finger? Yes, I remembered them jingling against the cup. Then I remembered that the shopping bags had been heavy and awkward, and that about a block from the store, the strap of my purse slipped off my shoulder and I had had to stop. I remembered putting my bags down on the hood of a parked car while I shifted the purse over my head to the other shoulder, school-satchel style, so it couldn't slip off. Then I picked everything up and resumed my way, only, perhaps I had not picked *everything* up? In addition to the shopping bags, I must have put my keys and my coffee mug down on the hood of the car, and perhaps, having slipped the coffee mug back onto my finger, I was deluded into thinking I had my keys – satisfied that I had slipped something over my finger. Then, I would have left my keys on the hood of that parked car on Fairmount Street.

It seemed too much to expect that the car would still be there, but I walked back over to where I remembered stopping. The car was gone, but even from half a block away I could see something lying on the curb, gleaming in the sun, right where the car had been. I came closer and there were my keys, waiting for me, winking. It's funny how vividly I remember this moment, the immense satisfaction of picking up my keys from the pavement. The squareness and rightness of my keys being *right there*, exactly where I'd figured I must have parted with them. A little feat of memory, a successful exercise of self-knowledge, proof that I could always recover what was important, even if I temporarily lost sight of it.

The children were happy with the newly painted table, and even happier when – having painted it – I was inspired to go out and buy four old Windsor-style chairs in a used furniture store, and to paint them the same colour. Our old chairs, a scruffy and mismatched assortment of leftovers, went out on the back porch. 'It's so nice in here now, Mummy,' said my son, 'like a *real* person's kitchen, like my friends' houses.' And I was a little shocked at this glimpse of how I'd been living, not noticing the shabbiness, unaware that my children noticed, calculated, compared.

Much has changed since then. My keys are not even the same keys, since I and my children now live in my friend's house, a few blocks away. My peach-coloured coffee mug broke, long before I moved. Since my friend had a perfectly good kitchen table set, a solid oak one that had belonged to his grandparents, there was no need for me to keep my pink table when we decided to live together; but I didn't want to part with it altogether, so it is now at my friend's chalet in the country. Sometimes when we go there I look at it and think about how painting it was the beginning of my being good to myself, after a long time of living numbly from day to day, in the wreckage of my failed marriage. The colour of it warms me, it is the colour I remember waking myself up with.

On Friday, too, when I discovered my keys were missing, I began going over my day step by step. I knew that this time I had not left my keys at home, because no one else had been home when I left the house, and I remembered locking up. I made sure the keys were not in my purse by turning it out onto my lap on the front steps, emptying everything; and by feeling along the seams of the lining for holes. Once or twice, I have thought my keys lost, only to find they had slipped through a hole in the lining, into the space between the purse leather and the liner. This time they had not.

Then I made a mental list of my errands: to the bank to deposit cheques, to the travel agency to pick up a train ticket, the grocery store for fresh fruit, the kosher bakery for braided challah loaves, back to the bank because I'd run out of cash, the corner store for milk. Theoretically, my keys could have been left in any of these places. It was also possible I had dropped them on the street. Dimly I thought I remembered walking along jingling my keys, calculating how many errands I had to do, and thinking it made more sense to put my keys away – slipping them into my purse as I walked. I did not quite see how, but my keys could have caught on the zipper somehow and fallen outside the bag, instead of falling into it. But wouldn't you think I'd have heard them fall? No, not necessarily. The traffic is loud along Park Avenue, and in addition, it being spring, pavement cutters were at work on several corners – I remembered wincing at the racket each time I passed them. There was nothing to do but retrace my whole route.

My keys were not at the bank. I remembered which tellers I had dealt with, Nelie and Brigitte, and I asked each of them directly. I checked the counter where I had filled out my deposit slips, and to make absolutely certain I asked the assistant manager as well. Nobody had turned in keys.

So I headed on to the travel agency. The name of it is Mazel, which means 'luck' in Hebrew – I think a nice name for a travel agency, we all hope for luck when we travel. It is run by a neighbourhood family of Hasidic Jews. Usually I book my train tickets at the station itself, but this time I had decided to try the travel agency because it is closer and more convenient. Now that I make short trips more and more frequently in connection with my work, it is sensible to have somewhere close by where I can make all the arrangements.

A very young, pretty Hasidic woman had undertaken to book my tickets earlier in the week, and I had picked them up from her that afternoon. I could tell that she was a married woman by her wig, which for some reason made her look even younger. She had smiled handing me my ticket, and had asked a little shyly what was the purpose of my trip; when I told her I was scheduled to give a talk, for my work, she wanted to know what was the subject of my talk and for whom was I working? I knew that for her, such inquiries constituted ordinary courtesy and were in no way intended to give offence. Had I told her I was Jewish, she would have wanted to know if I came from here, and who my parents were and where they came from, and whom I had married and how many children I had and so on. She would have asked me these things casually, with a lively familial interest, as if I were related.

As I walked back in that same direction in search of my keys, I passed many Hasidic families in the street, and I knew that the stir of activity, the speed and purpose with which they were moving, was because it was Friday and the Sabbath was approaching. I myself am Jewish, but I grew up in a home that was not religious, and I have never been observant in the strict tradition. Passing them I reflected briefly, as I often do walking these streets, on the differences between their lives and mine.

Remind me some day to describe to you the beauty of these families – the serenity and innocence of the young women's faces, the attractiveness of the children, dressed always so prettily; the quiet affection family members show towards one another, the gentle protectiveness with which very small children guide and oversee even smaller children. I do not know how people can speak ill of them, unless it is out of envy: they are so clearly happy and secure in their ways. My friend thinks that I romanticize them, but I see what I see. Yet I know that I myself could not live as they do, a life so circumscribed.

My friend is also Jewish; he grew up in a much more traditional home than mine, yet he, like my former husband, has let go of most of it, apparently without conflict. His last girlfriend, with whom he lived several years, was not Jewish. When we decided to live together, I asked him whether he wanted me to keep a kosher kitchen, but he only laughed and said gently, 'Why would you want to get into all that?' Nevertheless he is respectful of religious people, he does not need to justify himself by deriding them, as some do. Sometimes I see in his eyes a serenity that reminds me of theirs, an at-homeness in the world, and I think it is this above all that I love in him.

The travel agency is on the second floor, above a bank. Climbing the stairs I heard something that made my heart beat faster – I heard a jingling, as of keys. I thought, Someone right now has picked up my keys from that young woman's desk and is looking around to see who might have left them. But when I turned the corner below the landing, I saw a very large, tall Hasidic man closing and locking the doors of the office. He startled me a little, standing there at the top of the stairs in his black clothing, partly blocking the sunlight that filtered in through a dusty window.

I saw that the keys that he had in his hand were his own keys; they were not mine.

'Are you looking for somebody?' he asked me formally.

I said, 'I was here earlier today to pick up a train ticket. I lost my keys and I thought I might have left them here. Do you know if anybody found a set of keys?'

He shook his head. 'I don't think so,' he said. 'Who made you the ticket?'

I mentioned the woman by name.

'I think she would have told me, if she found something. She left half an hour ago,' he said. 'We close early on Friday. You can check again with her maybe next week?'

'All right,' I said, although I was sure that my keys were not there. I thought of wishing him a good Sabbath, but I did not want to complicate things for either of us by revealing that I was Jewish, so I only thanked him. As I started downstairs, he called after me, in a voice still formal but not unfriendly, 'I hope that you find them.'

My keys were not at the grocery store, the kosher bakery, or the corner store. They were not on the sidewalk; I kept my eyes peeled for them coming and going. Sometimes I had to stop and think: did I cross the street at this corner, or the next one? If my keys had fallen on the ground, it was important that I retrace my path exactly. But this time my good memory, my thoroughness, did not bear fruit. I did not find my keys. My keys were gone. Maybe they had fallen into a hole left by the pavement cutters. Maybe a child playing had found them lying on the pavement, and had carried them off somewhere – to a parent's safekeeping, or to be used in a childish game, or stored away with a child's treasures.

My keys were gone, and without reason I felt, for a moment, bereft and naked in the world.

I returned home hot and tired and a little upset with myself. My daughter was on the front steps, waiting for me. 'Mummy, where were you for so long? I was just going out to try to find you.'

'I lost my keys, and I had to go back and look for them,' I told her.

'And did you find them?'

'No,' I admitted.

'There, Mummy, you see,' she said. 'You tell us that you never lose your keys, but you do. So you shouldn't get so angry at us when we lose ours.'

Then she let me in with her keys, took the bag of challah loaves from me, and ran to set the Sabbath table, for even though I am not religious, I light candles on Friday evenings, I serve a Sabbath meal.

'I lost my keys,' I told my friend when he arrived home a few minutes later, and I waited for him to scold me for my carelessness; but he only came next to me and lightly kissed my forehead and tilted my chin upward so he could look into my face.

'Are you so upset about it, then?' he asked, affectionately, stroking the hair back from my forehead with gentle fingers.

'Only because I can't understand how it happened,' I replied, and then I was quiet, thinking about how easily one could have a new set of keys made, and how strange it was that one could feel such a keen disappointment, not to have found the old ones.

Robyn Sarah was born in New York City to Canadian parents, and has lived for most of her life in Montréal. A graduate of McGill University (where she majored in Philosophy and English) and of Québec's Conservatoire de Musique et d'Art Dramatique, she is the author of one previous collection of short stories, *A Nice Gazebo*, published by Véhicule Press in 1992. The same year, Anansi published *The Touchstone: Poems New and Selected*, a collection of her poetry spanning twenty years.